A POT O' GOLD

A Treasury of Irish Stories,
Poetry, Folklore,
and (of Course) Blarney

SELECTED AND ADAPTED BY
KATHLEEN KRULL

ILLUSTRATED BY
DAVID McPHAIL

Disney · HYPERION BOOKS
NEW YORK

Special thanks to John O'Connor
for creating the artwork for "Donald O'Neary and His Neighbors,"
all the display letters, the map of Ireland, and the border on page 83.
And thanks to Jan Waldron for creating the artwork for "Onions and Herrings."

To world travelers
Gery Greer and Bob Ruddick
—K.K.

For Alessandra, whose patience
and faith that I would someday finish
made it all possible
—D.McP.

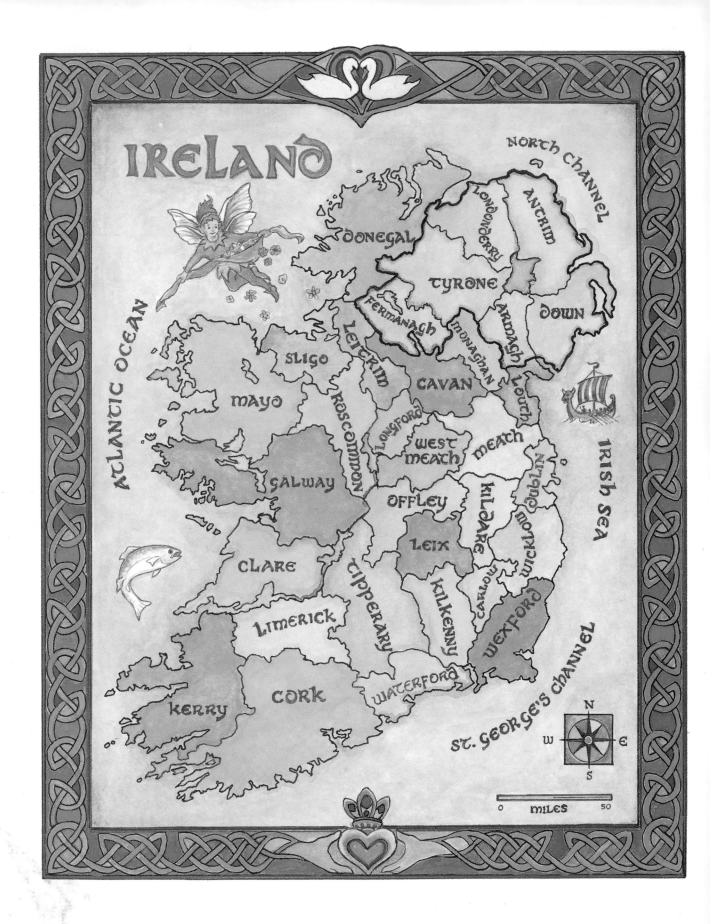

TABLE OF CONTENTS

Introduction /1

ONLY AN HOUR AWAY
The Sea

The Enchanted Cap /5

All Day I Hear the Noise of Waters *by James Joyce* /10

Herring Is King *by Alfred Percival Graves* /11

Saint Patrick and the Salmon /13

The Fate of the Children of Lir /17

Irish Lullaby *by Alfred Percival Graves* /22

NOT JUST POTATOES
The Food

Wheatlet, Son of Milklet /27

Bewitched Butter /31

Onions *and Herrings by Jonathan Swift* /35

The Potato /37

Irish Stew /38

Irish Soda Bread /39

Marshmallow Crackers /40

ALIVE-ALIVE-O
The Music

The Musician's Invitation /43

Larks *by Katherine Tynan* /44

Strings in the Earth and Air
by James Joyce /45

The Traveling Men of Ballycoo
by Eve Bunting /47

Cockles and Mussels (Molly Malone) /54

The Fairies' Dancing Place /57

EMERALD ISLE
The Pride

Saint Bridget Spreads Her Cloak /61

The Limerick Lasses *by Alfred Percival Graves* /63

Finn McCool and the Scottish Giant /65

The Land of Eternal Youth /71

Ireland *by Dora Sigerson* /75

Irish Battle Cries /77

Irish Blessings /78

All Things Bright and Beautiful *by Cecil Frances Alexander* /80

IN LOVE WITH WORDS
The Scholars

The Irish Student and His Cat / 85

Ode to Writers *by Arthur O'Shaughnessy* / 87

Where My Books Go *by William Butler Yeats* / 89

The Man Who Had No Story / 91

FIELDS AND FARMS
The Land

The Wind That Shakes the Barley
by Katherine Tynan / 97

Donald O'Neary and His Neighbors / 101

The Lake Isle of Innisfree
by William Butler Yeats / 106

My Land *by Thomas Davis* / 108

ENCHANTMENT
The Fairies

The Fairies in New Ross / 113

The Fairies *by William Allingham* / 114

Fair, Brown, and Trembling / 119

The Stolen Child *by William Butler Yeats* / 127

To Cure a Child Under a Fairy Spell / 131

The Star-Child *by Oscar Wilde* / 133

WHO MAKES THE FAIRIES' SHOES?
The Leprechauns

Patrick O'Donnell and the Leprechaun / 147

The Leprechaun *by William Allingham* / 152

The Leprechaun *by Robert Dwyer Joyce* / 154

PEOPLE NEVER STOP TALKING
The Blarney

What It Is, How to Do It, and the Blarney Stone / 159

Limericks / 161

Brian O'Linn / 163

Folk Riddles / 166

A Riddle *by Jonathan Swift* / 167

Irish Oaths and Curses / 168

The Curse *by John Millington Synge* / 169

Ancient Irish Folk Cures / 171

Philosophies for the Very Young *by Oscar Wilde* / 173

Source Notes / 175

Acknowledgments / 182

INTRODUCTION

RELAND LOVES WORDS—"more lasting than the wealth of the world," according to one old proverb. In the courts of the ancient Irish kings, poets actually ranked above warriors. (And warriors were *required* to be witty.) Ireland's past and present bubble over with myths, legends, poetry, ballads, and wordplay of all kinds.

The challenge in bringing such a treasure trove to young readers was to not create a book too heavy to lift. Searching through lots of dusty volumes to find the very best—some things perhaps familiar, some things a bit of a stretch—that was the fun part. These selections and their adaptations represent a balance between material that is child-friendly and as true as possible to the original sources. . . .

All with the intention of helping to keep Ireland's glorious cultural heritage alive.

Cead mille failte, mo chara!

Which is Irish for "A hundred thousand welcomes, my friend!"

—Kathleen Krull
(whose grandparents came from
county Kerry and county Roscommon)

ONLY AN HOUR AWAY
The Sea

For thousands of years, people considered Ireland the edge
of the known world. Water defines it. The ocean pounds at
every side of this small island, approximately the size of the
state of Maine. Wherever you stand, you are only about
an hour away from the sea, or even closer to one of the
island's eight hundred rivers or lakes.

THE ENCHANTED CAP

Once you've seen the wild Irish coast, and the whales and dolphins
swimming near it, it is not hard to believe in the existence of sea fairies.
The shore is like a doorway to another world, a mysterious kingdom under
the waves, where the rulers are merrow, merfolk, selkies—sea fairies all.
This bittersweet mermaid tale has many variations.

ONG AGO, IN THE village of Gollerus,
lived a fisherman named Dick Fitzgerald.

He stayed alone in a stone cottage above the
shore, with nothing but seagulls for company. In the long winter
evenings he would smoke his pipe by the peat fire and watch the
blue smoke curling. And sometimes, when the wind rustled the grass
outside, he seemed to hear a voice sighing his name.

One evening, the men of the village were bringing their boats
full of herring onto shore. Homeward they hurried, to warm places
where their wives were setting out lights.

Dick Fitzgerald was the last to drag his boat up on shore and
hoist the string of fish upon his back. Then, as he turned, he saw a
glimmer of white in the shadows of the rocks. Between birds' cries
he heard high laughter. He set down his fish and carefully stepped
toward the rocks, hardly daring to breathe.

Hiding behind the largest rock, he saw seven women with long flowing hair, white as swans, dancing in a circle amid the waves. And he saw a pile of red caps heaped on a boulder nearby. Now he knew that they were mermaids, who in the sea are seals, but near land take off their enchanted caps and appear as women.

Dick Fitzgerald crept toward the pile of caps and slid the top one down. The dance stopped, and the women raced to the boulder and slipped on their caps. Shiny brown seals slithered back into the foam.

All but one. She stood before him as white as pearl, her sea-green hair shining in the night. She stared at him with great dark eyes, then said in a trembling voice, "Oh, Man, please give me back my cap."

He took a step toward her and grasped her outstretched arm. "Come with me, Fish," he said gently, "and I will make you Mistress Fitzgerald."

All the village came to the wedding of Dick Fitzgerald and the mermaid. Six sheep were roasted, and Fitzgerald clapped his hands to the music of fiddle and pipe. The woman sat quietly, listening to private music of her own.

Thirteen summers passed, and she bore him two children, a boy and a girl. They had the sandy hair of their father, but the dark eyes of their mother, and there were little webs of clear skin between their fingers and toes. Each day, when Dick was out in his boat, the mermaid and her children would wander the shore to gather shells. In May, when the air smelled of roses and the children danced around her, she seemed almost happy. But during storms she grew restless and moved about the house as if pulled by unseen tides.

One afternoon, as she knelt digging up roots to roast for supper, the voice of her daughter rang through the salty air: "Look, I found the strangest thing in an old fishing net."

Her mother rose to her feet and touched the red cap. With one arm around her daughter, she called her son, and spoke softly: "Soon

you will not see me again in the shape I am in now. As much as I love you, I must become myself again."

That night, as the moon rose, the mermaid left her sleeping husband and walked alone to the shore. Lightly she stepped over the rocks, holding her red cap. She took one last look at the cottage. Then she donned her cap and dropped into the water.

A sleek brown head streamed toward the horizon, and then, leaping and diving, came six other seals. They formed a circle around her, and then all were lost in the night.

Dick Fitzgerald stirred and called for his wife. The only answer was the rustle of grass outside.

Year after year, he waited for her to return. But she never did.

Except on nights when the moon was young, and his children would not sleep, but ran down to the sands on silent webbed feet. There, by the rocks, they waited for a speckled brown seal with great dark eyes. Laughing and calling her name, they splashed into the foaming water and swam with her until dawn.

ALL DAY I HEAR
THE NOISE OF WATERS

James Joyce

In this poem, the sound of the sea is not always happy. James Joyce,
world-famous for *Ulysses,* *A Portrait of the Artist as a Young Man,*
and *Finnegan's Wake,* was born in Dublin in 1882. He married Nora
Barnacle from Galway, wrote about Dublin his whole life, and died in 1941.

All day I hear the noise of waters
Making moan,
Sad as the sea bird is, when going
Forth alone,
He hears the winds cry to the waters'
Monotone.

The gray winds, the cold winds are blowing
Where I go.
I hear the noise of many waters
Far below.
All day, all night, I hear them flowing
To and fro.

HERRING IS KING

Alfred Percival Graves

The sea means fish, and this poem sings the praises of one in particular.
Alfred Percival Graves was born in Dublin in 1846, son of the bishop of
Limerick, father of the poet Robert Graves. He worked as an inspector of
schools, became secretary and president of the Irish Literary Society,
wrote many volumes of poetry, and died in 1931.

> Let all the fish that swim the sea,
> Salmon and turbot, cod and ling,
> Bow down the head and bend the knee
> To herring, their king! to herring, their king!

SAINT PATRICK
AND THE SALMON

Ireland's patron saint arrived in 432 as a sixteen-year-old slave kidnapped by pirates. After six years of tending sheep in county Antrim, he escaped and dedicated himself to establishing monasteries throughout Ireland. We know few facts about Patrick, but we can be sure that he must have radiated courage—he was one of the few people to stand up to fierce Irish chieftains and survive. He died in 461 and was buried in county Armagh. We celebrate the day of his death, March 17, as St. Patrick's Day. Myths shroud Patrick—such as, did he really banish snakes from Ireland (and were snakes ever there)? This is one such myth, about the fish of knowledge—the salmon.

 T WAS ST. PATRICK who gave the salmon its power to jump, and he who twisted the mouth of the flounder. It happened in just this way.

Patrick baptized a great many people, except for those unbelievers who refused to have anything to do with him. One day, he passed by a river where some men were fishing. They were unbelievers who decided to have some fun with the saint.

One of the fishermen shouted, "Hold on, Patrick, and we'll get you a fish!"

"Thank you," said Patrick, and he sat down by the river. One of the fishermen pulled up a huge fish. Then he threw it into the basket along with the other fish. Patrick stood up, and another fisherman called, "Wait! You'll get the next fish we catch."

"I will indeed," said Patrick. He sat down again.

Soon they reeled in another fish, but they threw it into the basket again.

Patrick was about to leave when a third fisherman said, "We promise, the very next fish!"

"Of course," Patrick said, and sat down once more.

Now, the first fish they caught was a flounder. Until that time, the head of the flounder was as straight on its body as the head of any other fish. But when the flounder saw the unbelievers mocking the saint, it wanted to join in. It looked backward and twisted its mouth to sneer at Patrick.

"May your head remain as it is!" said Patrick.

The flounder was unable to get rid of its twisted mouth and neck, and so they have remained ever since.

Just as Patrick was about to leave for once and for all, a salmon leaped cleanly out of the river and landed in his lap.

"I give you the gift of jumping," Patrick said.

And ever since, the salmon can jump better than any other fish, and that will be true until the end of time.

THE FATE
OF THE
CHILDREN OF LIR

Stepmothers are not always wicked and the sea is not always sad, but they are in this haunting legend. It goes back two thousand years, to the oldest Irish myths—about the Tuatha De Danann, a race of gods founded by the goddess Danu. They traveled on a cloud to settle in Ireland, which they ruled by magic. Eventually they were defeated, but they live on invisibly, as fairies.

 LONG TIME AGO, in the age of gods and heroes, there lived in Ireland those who looked human but had the powers of gods. Lir, the sea god, married the daughter of the king of the gods. She gave birth to one daughter, Fingula, and three sons: Aed, and the twins Fiachra and Conn.

Then she died, and Lir mourned. If not for love for his children he would have died, too. He wanted them to have a new mother, so he married his wife's sister.

At first the stepmother felt affection for the children, and indeed everyone who saw them could not help loving them. Lir doted upon the four, and they always slept in beds in front of his own.

Then jealousy overtook his new wife, and soon she went mad with it.

She couldn't bring herself to kill them, but she took them to the

Lake of the Red Eye. With a wand she stole from a Druid (a pre-Christian priest), she transformed them into four beautiful, perfectly white swans floating upon the shimmering lake.

"Away from me, you children of Lir," she called.

In vain did the four swans, especially Fingula, cry and beg her to break the spell.

Instead, the stepmother chanted, "Never shall you be free until a woman from the south be united to a man from the north. Nine hundred years shall you wander the lakes and streams of Erin. This only I will grant you: that you keep your own speech, and no music in the world shall equal the sad music you sing."

Then she fled, already sorry for the evil she had done. The lies she told Lir about where his children were did not convince him, and he immediately set out for the lake.

As Lir came to the shore he saw the swans sailing toward him, speaking with human voices. Fingula sang to him and told all that happened.

Lir began to weep uncontrollably.

Conn begged his father to help. "Make us as we were. We want to run and play!"

Lir went to the hall of the king for help. In agony, Lir and the king agreed they could not change the children back because the enchantment was binding for nine hundred years.

But the King proclaimed throughout Erin that no swan should be killed from now on. And he summoned the stepmother to the hall and transformed her into a huge bat. With a shriek, she rose up into a black cloud and was never seen again.

The four swans fled the Lake of the Red Eye, soaring lightly, singing. They stayed all alone, filled with cold and regret. Instead of their pleasant life as children of Lir, they now had white sand and briny water for food and drink, and bare rocks for beds.

One night a fierce storm came up, and Fingula said, "Brothers, let us choose where to meet if the winds separate us." They agreed on the Rock of the Seals.

Then the waves swelled. The thunder roared, the lightning flashed, and the storm raged over the great sea, scattering the children of Lir.

In the calm afterward, Fingula flew to the Rock of the Seals, where all night she waited. "Woe upon me that I am alive!" she crooned. "My wings are frozen to my sides. O beloved three, O beloved three. . . ."

At the rising of the sun, she finally saw Conn coming toward her with drenched feathers, and Fiachra also. They were too cold and faint to say a word, but she nestled them under the shelter of her wings and said, "If Aed could come to us now, our happiness would be complete." And soon he was there, and Fingula put him under the feathers of her breast, and Fiachra under her right wing, and Conn under her left.

The years rolled by, and the children suffered loneliness and fear. The cries of shipwrecked sailors haunted them, monsters of the deep terrified them, and bitter winters nearly froze them. Love for each other was all that they had.

Once, during their travels, they came near the palace of their father, Lir. But when they flew overhead, they saw nothing but green raths (circles of dirt believed to be fairy forts) and forest—no house, no hounds, no welcoming fire, no one to greet them.

The four lamented in song: "Now has come the greatest of our pain—there lives no one who knows us."

So they flew to the Lake of the Birds. They made their home beside a little church and were beloved for their beautiful singing.

The years passed, and it happened that a princess from the south of Ireland was to wed a prince from the north. The princess had heard about the wondrous birds, and she insisted on having them sing at the wedding. The prince went to seize the birds, but as soon as he laid hands on them, their feathery coats fell off.

The prince fled in terror. The snowy white swans withered into four bony old people without blood or flesh—and soon without life.

But the children of Lir had found peace at last. They were

buried, with Fiachra and Conn on either side of Fingula, and Aed in her arms.

The days of gods and heroes were gone forever.

IRISH LULLABY
Alfred Percival Graves

When the sea isn't sad or cold, it can be a comfort.
Babies have a special connection to the Irish seas when lulled to sleep
with nonsense syllables that imitate the waves.

I'd rock my own sweet childie to rest in a cradle of gold on a
    bough of the willow,
To the *shoheen ho* of the wind of the west and the *lulla lo* of the
    soft sea billow.
Sleep, baby dear, sleep without fear,
Mother is here beside your pillow.

I'd put my own sweet childie to sleep in a silver boat on the
    beautiful river,
Where a *shoheen* whisper the white cascades, and a *lulla lo* the
    green flags shiver.
Sleep, baby dear, sleep without fear,
Mother is here with you forever.

Lulla lo! to the rise and fall of mother's soft skin 'tis sleep has
    bound you,
And O my child, what cozier nest for rosier rest could love have
    found you?
Sleep, baby dear, sleep without fear,
Mother's two arms are clasped around you.

NOT JUST POTATOES
The Food

In the past, Ireland has been a poor island,
with food always scarce. Small wonder that many of its
poems and stories celebrate things to eat.

WHEATLET, SON OF MILKLET

This nonsense poem is purely about things to eat.
Speaking are gluttonous giants living in an imaginary country
called Guzzledom amid mountains of lard.

Wheatlet, son of Milklet,
Son of juicy Bacon,
    Is mine own name.
Honeyed Butter-roll
Is the man's name
    That bears my bag.

Haunch of Mutton
Is my dog's name,
    Of lovely leaps.

Lard, my wife,
Sweetly smiles
    Across the brose.*

Cheese-curds, my daughter,
Goes round the spit,
    Fair is her fame.

*Porridge

Corned Beef is my son,
Who beams over a cloak,
    Enormous, of fat.

Savour of Savours
Is the name of my wife's maid:
Morning-early
Across New-milk Lake she went.

Beef-lard, my steed,
An excellent stallion
    That increases studs;
A guard against toil
Is the saddle of cheese
    Upon his back.

A large necklace of delicious cheese-curds
    Around his back;
His halter and his traces all
    Of fresh butter.

BEWITCHED BUTTER

So important was butter—and magic—that almost every Irish village
has a version of this tale.

RIAN AND PEG HANLON'S cows were
the finest for miles around. Their milk and butter were
the richest and sweetest, and brought the highest
price at every market.

Things went well until one season when the cows, for no visi-
ble reason, grew thin. Soon they were scarcely able to crawl around
their pasture. The small quantity of milk some of them continued to
supply was so bitter that even the pigs would not drink it, while the
butter it produced stunk so horribly that the very dogs would not
eat it.

The unfortunate Hanlons were completely bewildered. They
tried every remedy they could think of, but in vain. Ruin stared them
in the face, and they became moody and sleepless. Brian wandered
about the fields among his stricken cattle like a madman.

One hot evening in July, Peg was sitting at her door, spinning
at her wheel, in a gloomy state of mind. Coming down the narrow
green lane she saw a barefoot woman enveloped in a scarlet cloak.

"God bless this house and all belonging to it," said the stranger
as Peg ran and fetched a chair. "I am dry with the heat. Can you give

me a drink?" She appeared of great age, her forehead etched with a thousand wrinkles, her long gray hair falling in matted locks from beneath a white linen cap.

"I have nothing to offer except water," replied the farmer's wife.

"Are you not the owner of the cattle I see yonder?" said the old hag.

Peg briefly related what was happening with the cows.

"Have you any of the milk in the house?" the hag asked. "Show me."

Peg filled a jug and handed it over. No sooner did the old woman taste the milk than she spat it out. Just then Brian walked in.

"Neighbor," said the stranger, "your wife says your cattle are going against you. Why have you not sought a cure?"

"I have sought a cure until I was heartbroken, and they get worse every day."

"What will you give me if I cure them for you?"

"Anything in our power," replied Brian and his wife in one breath.

"First, lock the door," said the hag. "Now, take this milk and set it to boil on the fire. Into the pan put nine straight pins so new they have never been used in clothes."

They did as she told them, and the nine shiny pins soon began to simmer in the bitter milk. The hag stirred them, at the same time singing some verses in a low, wild voice. She grew quite pale, she gnashed her teeth, her hand trembled, and she began to seem other than human.

As the hour of twelve o'clock arrived, a loud wail was heard approaching the house. The old woman stopped her chanting.

"Let me in!" The crying voice was now at the door, and a violent knocking followed.

"'Tis the villain who has your cattle bewitched!" shouted the hag.

Brian unbarred the door to find a red-haired woman whose piercing yells were hurting their ears. She was a neighbor by the name of Grace Dogherty. She had five or six cows, but neighbors noticed she sold more butter than other farmers' wives who had twenty. Brian had, from the beginning, suspected her of having something to do with his misfortune, but with no proof, he had held his peace.

"Oh, please, take that cruel pan off the fire," the woman screeched in agony. "Take out those cruel pins. They're piercing holes in my heart! Take them out, and I promise I'll never touch the milk of your cows again!"

With a grim smile, the hag took the milk off the fire. Brian and Peg pressed her to accept some payment for her services, but she refused. She remained a few days at their house, then departed, no one knew whither.

As for Grace, when her fate became known, her family was so ashamed, they left for America.

O N I O N S   A N D   H E R R I N G S
Jonathan Swift

Calls from women selling fruits and vegetables on the street inspired
Jonathan Swift to write these verses. Swift, born in Dublin in 1667,
was Dean of St. Patrick's Cathedral in Dublin, wrote *Gulliver's Travels*
and other works, and became known as an Irish national hero. At his death
in 1745, he left his fortune to found a mental hospital in Dublin.

Come, follow me by the smell,
Here are the delicate onions to sell;
I promise to use you well.
They make the blood warmer,
You'll feed like a farmer;

For this is every cook's opinion,
No savory dish without an onion;
But, lest your kissing should be spoiled,
Your onions must be thoroughly boiled:

Or else you may spare
Your mistress a share,
The secret will never be known:
She cannot discover
The breath of her lover,
But think it is as sweet as her own.

Be not sparing,
Leave off swearing.
Buy my herring
Fresh from Malahide,*
Better never was tried.
Come, eat them with pure fresh butter and mustard,
Their bellies are soft, and as white as a custard.
Come, sixpence a dozen, to get me some bread,
Or, like my own herrings, I soon shall be dead.

*A town near Dublin

THE POTATO

Ireland *is* famous for the potato. So important was it that when a mysterious disease rotted the potato beds in 1845, Ireland suffered. Within ten years, a third of its people either died or left for America. Today Ireland is the most sparsely populated country in Europe—and the United States has some 44 million Irish-Americans.

Sublime potatoes! that, from Antrim's shore
To famous Kerry, form the poor man's store;
Agreeing well with every place and state—
The peasant's noggin, or the rich man's plate.
Much prized when smoking from the teeming pot,
Or in turf-embers roasted crisp and hot.
Welcome, although you be our only dish;
Welcome, companion to flesh, fowl, or fish;
But to the real gourmands, the learned few,
Most welcome, steaming in an Irish stew.

IRISH STEW

4 large onions, cut in wedges

2 tablespoons oil

5 large carrots, cut in thick slices

1 ½ pounds steak or lamb

6 large potatoes

1 cup water

Salt and pepper to taste

Brown onions in oil in a pot. Add carrots and cook for a few minutes. Cut meat into ¼- to ½-inch cubes and add to pot. Wash, peel, and slice potatoes and add to pot. Pour in water, season to taste with salt and pepper, and bring to a boil. Reduce heat and simmer over low heat until meat and vegetables are tender. The stew can be thickened by mixing 2 tablespoons flour with a little water and adding it to the stew. Heat until thickened and serve piping hot. Serves six.

IRISH SODA BREAD

Today Ireland's population is growing, not shrinking, and becoming famous for all sorts of foods. But all over the country you will still be served this traditional sweet bread.

4 cups flour

1 cup sugar

4 teaspoons baking powder

1/2 teaspoon salt

1 stick butter, melted

1 1/2 cups raisins

2 tablespoons caraway seeds

1 egg, slightly beaten

1 1/2 cups buttermilk

1/3 teaspoon baking soda

In a large mixing bowl, combine the flour, sugar, salt, and baking powder. Cut in butter. Stir in raisins and caraway seeds. In a smaller bowl, mix the egg, buttermilk, and baking soda. Pour into large bowl and mix well. Shape the dough into a ball and place on a buttered baking sheet. Flatten the ball into an 8- or 9-inch loaf. Cut a cross into the loaf to mark into quarters. Brush with melted butter and bake in a preheated 375-degree oven for an hour, or until golden brown.

MARSHMALLOW CRACKERS

Cream crackers were invented in Ireland, but graham crackers
or another plain, unsalty cracker will do.

10 marshmallows
10 cream crackers
10 blobs of butter
10 almonds

Put a marshmallow on top of each cracker. Put a small piece of
butter on each marshmallow, topped by an almond. Place on a pan
and put under broiler until marshmallow has melted over all.

ALIVE~ALIVE~O
The Music

THE MUSICIAN'S
INVITATION

I am of Ireland
      And of the holy land
      Of Ireland.

Good sir, I pray thee,
For the sake of charity,
Come and dance with me,
In Ireland.

*Fragment of an Old English dance song
composed by a 14th-century minstrel*

LARKS

Katherine Tynan

Katherine Tynan (1861~1931) was born in Dublin, attended convent school, and started to write poetry in her teens. While raising three children, and despite being half blind, she wrote eighteen volumes of poetry, 105 novels, and much else.

All day in exquisite air
The song clomb an invisible stair,
Flight on flight, story on story,
Into the dazzling glory.

There was no bird, only a singing,
Up in the glory, climbing and ringing,
Like a small golden cloud at even,
Trembling 'twixt earth and heaven.

I saw no staircase winding, winding,
Up in the dazzle, sapphire and blinding,
Yet round by round, in exquisite air,
The song went up the stair.

STRINGS
IN THE
EARTH AND AIR

James Joyce

Strings in the earth and air
    Make music sweet;
Strings by the river where
    The willows meet.

There's music along the river,
    For Love wanders there,
Pale flowers on his mantle,
    Dark leaves on his hair.

All softly playing,
    With head to the music bent,
And fingers straying
    Upon an instrument.

THE TRAVELING MEN
OF BALLYCOO

Eve Bunting

This premier Irish-American author, born in 1928, left Belfast for California
in 1958. Among her several hundred books for children is this tale honoring
Ireland's musicians. She started writing it one day on the concert program
as she was sitting in the audience enjoying that great traditional
Irish group, the Chieftains.

 ATHAL, SEAN, AND JIMMY O'Malley were
the Traveling Men, and there were those who said
they were maybe the greatest Traveling Men that
Ireland had ever seen.

They had no place that they called home, though Simey Rooney
had left them a cottage in Ballycoo when he passed on. No matter.
The whole length of the land was theirs, for they were the
Traveling Men, taking their songs and music with them wherever
they'd go.

Cathal played the penny whistle. He had a tune called "The
Hunt," and in it you could hear, plain as day, the high, wild keen of
the hunting horn and the gallop of horses and the bark of dogs as
they lit out after the hare. There'd be the sounds of hounds yelping
and slavering and, in the end, the terrible squeal of the murdered
hare, real enough and true enough to chill the blood in your body.

47

There was many a man heard Cathal play and hung up his boots to hunt no more.

Sean played the fiddle, bent near in two over the top of himself, every bit of him jigging to his music. He'd fiddle so mightily that the rosin he rubbed on his bow rose and hung like a mist around his head.

Young Jimmy played the melodeon. He had a tune, a march it was, and you could have sworn a whole brigade of pipers was tramping over the nearest hill, three abreast, their kilts blowing around their bare red knees. All of that came out of a box thing no bigger than a penny loaf.

None of the three was for marriage. Didn't they have all they needed in each other, with their music to share and a royal welcome wherever they went?

Cathal always had the right word for everything. "It's the great life we have," he said. "We're taking joy and spreading it from place to place and leaving it behind us when we go. What more could a man ask?"

"Nothing," Sean said.

"Nothing," Young Jimmy agreed.

Maybe it was too great to last forever. It seemed to the Traveling Men afterward that the years had gone by without their noticing them.

Sean was the first to take bad, with the pains in his back.

Cathal and Young Jimmy got a fine gray donkey by the name of Mrs. Murphy to carry him. She had eyes, big and shiny as two licked stones, and a back as wide as the valleys between the Mourne Mountains.

When Cathal got the aches in his two legs, Mrs. Murphy was fit enough to hold both him and Sean, and Young Jimmy helped them on and off her back.

The people were still glad to see the Traveling Men. Weren't they the same good boys they'd always been and wasn't their music as fine as ever? They'd be invited in and given mugs of tea. Mrs. Murphy had a corner to herself, and there was always a blanket for Cathal's legs and another for Sean's back and a jar of homemade liniment for them to take along when the music was done for the day and the Traveling Men moved on.

But it was getting harder for them to move on. It was getting harder for them to move.

"There's nothing for it but to settle down," Cathal said. "We'll stop traveling and live in one place, same as everyone else. We're not that young anymore."

Which was true. Even Young Jimmy was close to seventy, and he'd lost half of his good, strong teeth.

"It's called making the best of a bad job," Cathal said. Cathal always had the right word for everything.

So they went to Ballycoo.

Simey Rooney's cottage was tight and dry. They settled into it like old birds into a warm nest. In time, they got for themselves a big, soft dog that they called Red Rory and a cow called Maggie and it was surprising how good everything was.

But the evenings were the best. Sean would take out his fiddle and rosin up his bow, Cathal would blow a tender breath into his penny whistle, and Jimmy's bent fingers would dance across his melodeon. The notes flew around their heads like quick, white moths, taking away every ache. The fire sparked up the chimney, and Red Rory slept in its warmth. They'd play "Long Slender Sally" and "The Dark Woman of the Glen," and sometimes Red Rory would beat his whiskery tail on the floor and smile in his sleep while the slow, sweet dusk came settling into night.

They were good times to be sure. But there was something wanting.

It was Cathal who put the word to it.

"It's right and fine us playing for ourselves and getting the good of it. But we're used to sharing the music we make, and it's not ever as sweet when it's kept to ourselves."

They thought about it, but it was Young Jimmy who had the idea to hang the paper on the door. It said:

MUSIC NIGHTLY
Come and be Welcome

"We'll wait now and see what transpires," Cathal said.

They didn't have long to wait. That very night there came a knock on the door. There were three children outside.

"We heard you playing and we read your notice. Can we come in a wee while and listen?"

"Indeed, and we're glad to have you," Sean told them, and that was that.

Soon the word got out that the greatest Traveling Men that ever were had come to rest in Ballycoo, and there was never a night without music and friends to savor it.

"It's better now, isn't it?" Young Jimmy asked Cathal.

"Aye. Now it's complete," Cathal said.

Sometimes they'd push the settle and stools against the wall and there'd be stepping to "Big John's Reel."

Sometimes there'd be music just for the listening, bringing fairies into the wee warm room . . . or storms at sea with waves so fierce you were afeared of drowning.

Sometimes you'd be in a forest with the birds singing their shining songs, or you'd be in India, the snake charmer piping his snake like a rope from its curly basket.

One night, when their visitors had gone, the Traveling Men lay side by side in their three feather beds. Rain beat on the outside thatch, and the room was warm with the smell of liniment.

"Since we travel no more, we can't very well be called the Traveling Men, now can we, Cathal?" Jimmy asked sleepily. "What should be the name for us now?"

Cathal scratched at his beard. "Don't we go places every night of our lives, and don't we take all here along with us? Traveling Men we were and are still and always will be."

Young Jimmy smiled and closed his eyes. Cathal always had the right word for everything.

COCKLES AND MUSSELS
(MOLLY MALONE)

This ballad has become Dublin's unofficial anthem, crooned at football games and not very seriously. It started out sad, a lament for a fish seller who harvested shellfish from Dublin's beaches and sold them on the street until she died in a cholera epidemic.

In Dublin's fair city,
Where girls are so pretty,
I first set my eyes on sweet Molly Malone,
As she pushed her wheelbarrow
Through streets broad and narrow,
Crying, "Cockles and mussels, alive, alive oh!"

CHORUS: *Alive, alive oh! alive, alive oh!*
Crying, "Cockles and mussels, alive, alive oh!"

Now, she was a fishmonger,
And sure 'twas no wonder,
For so were her mother and father before,
And they each wheeled their barrow,
Through streets broad and narrow,
Crying, "Cockles and mussels, alive, alive oh!"
CHORUS

She died of a fever,

And no one could save her,

And that was the end of sweet Molly Malone.

Now her ghost wheels her barrow,

Through streets broad and narrow,

Crying, "Cockles and mussels, alive, alive oh!"

CHORUS

THE FAIRIES'
DANCING PLACE

One thing you do not want to mess with is a circle of stones around a heap of
dirt—the rath where the fairies dance. Raths crop up in pastures all over
Ireland, and smart farmers never plow them for fear of disturbing
the fairies and bringing bad luck.

ANTY McCLUSKEY had married a wife, and,
of course, it was necessary to have a house in which to
keep her. Lanty had a bit of a farm, about six acres,
and on it he decided to build a house. To make it as comfortable as
possible, he selected as its site one of those beautiful green circles
that are supposed to be the playground of the fairies.

Now, Lanty was warned against this. But he was a headstrong
man, not much given to fear, and he said he would not give up such
a pleasant site for his house to oblige all the fairies in Europe. He
proceeded with the building, which he finished off very neatly.
And, as it is usual on these occasions to give one's neighbors and
friends a housewarming, Lanty, after bringing home the wife in the
morning, got a fiddler and threw a dance in the evening.

The music and hilarity were proceeding nicely, when a noise
was heard after night had set in. It was like a straining of ribs and

rafters on the top of the house. The folks assembled all listened to the crushing and heaving and groaning and panting, as if a thousand little men were pulling down the roof.

"Come," said a voice in a tone of command, "work hard—we must have Lanty's house down before midnight."

This was an unwelcome bit of news to Lanty. Unable to fight such enemies, he announced: "Gentle fairies, I humbly ask your pardon for building on any place belonging to you. But if you'll let me dance here this night, I'll pull the house down tomorrow."

A noise like the slapping of a thousand tiny little hands, a shout of "Bravo, Lanty! Build halfway between the two white thorns on the hill above," another hearty little shout, a brisk rushing noise—and they were heard of no more.

But the story does not end here. For Lanty, when digging the foundation of his new house, found a pot of gold. So that in leaving the fairies their dancing place, he became a richer man than had he never come in contact with them at all.

EMERALD ISLE
The Pride

SAINT BRIDGET SPREADS HER CLOAK

Of all the saints crowding Ireland's history, the next best known after
St. Patrick is St. Bridget of Kildare (about 453-523). She is said to have
established a religious community noted for the learning of its nuns and monks.
Bridget is celebrated each February 1. Legends about her include her weaving
the first piece of cloth in Ireland, creating the Lake of Milk to feed
visiting bishops, and this one.

 FTEN DID BRIDGET argue with a rich man
who owned all the land around. He would not help
the poor as much as she thought he should. Finally,
one day, almost as a joke, she begged, "At least grant me as much land
as it would take my cloak to cover."

"I will give that," he agreed, mainly to get rid of her.

So she laid down her cloak, and directed four of her sisters to
spread it out. Instead of laying it flat, each nun took a corner and
faced a different point of the compass. They started running. Other
holy women joined them, seizing pieces to make the cloak into a
circle spreading out miles and miles in all directions.

"Oh, St. Bridget," said the frightened landowner, "what are
you doing?"

"Covering your whole property to punish you for your
stinginess."

"This will never do! What if I give you a decent plot of land, and promise to be more generous in the future?"

The saint smiled, and if the man ever again tightened his purse strings, she had only to remind him of her miraculous cloak.

THE LIMERICK LASSES

Alfred Percival Graves

Ireland has a tradition of mighty women, from its last two elected presidents
(Mary Robinson and Mary McAleese)
to the legendary girls from county Limerick.

O Limerick dear,
　　　It's far and it's near
I've travelled the round of this circular sphere;
　　　Still an' all to my mind
　　　No colleens you'll find
As lovely and modest, as merry and kind,
　　　As our Limerick lasses;
　　　Our Limerick lasses—
So lovely and modest, so merry and kind.
　　　　So row,
　　　　Strong and slow,
Chorusing after me as we go:—
　　　Still an' all to my mind
　　　No colleens you'll find
As lovely and modest, as merry and kind,
　　　As our Limerick lasses;
　　　Our Limerick lasses—
So lovely and modest, so merry and kind.

FINN McCOOL AND THE SCOTTISH GIANT

The Fianna, or Fenians, were a mythical heroic army of Irish warriors. Trained by a legendary woman warrior named Fiachel, their greatest leader was Finn McCool. Over the course of 2,000 years of Fenian tales, Finn was sometimes a magical warrior-hero—a wise poet as well as daring fighter—and sometimes a less noble clown-trickster. But always he was larger than life, a Hercules or Paul Bunyan kind of guy. Knockmany is in Ulster, and "The Giant's Causeway" is a real place—a bizarre formation of rocky columns along the northern coast. This eerie moonscape was caused by volcanic eruptions. (Or else was the work of giants . . .)

IN ALL OF IRELAND, there was no giant as big or brave as Finn McCool. Everyone knew about him, his glorious deeds, his giant wife Oona, and the marvelous thumb of knowledge he gained after touching a salmon. Whenever Finn sucked his thumb, he could see anything happening in Ireland, even in the future.

Now, Finn and some of his huge friends were hard at work constructing a bridge from Ireland to Scotland, across what was known as the Giant's Causeway. One day a messenger arrived with the news that Far Rua was looking for Finn, calling for a fight.

Finn decided he had to see how his wife was, and he had to do it right then.

Why? Because, just by walking around, the Scottish giant Far Rua made little earthquakes. Because he once flattened a thunderbolt with one blow, and he kept it in his pocket like a pancake, as a souvenir. Because he had a magic finger, too—his middle finger made him the biggest, strongest giant in Scotland, and he had defeated every giant in Ireland—except Finn.

Finn wasted no time in yanking a fir tree out of the ground and chopping off its roots and branches to make a walking stick. Then he took off for his home at the top of Knockmany Hill.

Oona welcomed him with such a playful smack that it curled the waters of the lake at the bottom of the hill. "You darling bully!" she cried.

"And how is my little bilberry?" replied Finn with a kiss heard one town over.

But he could keep up his good humor for only so long, and within minutes he was confessing his dread of Far Rua. "How to manage, I don't know," he worried. "If I run away, I am disgraced, and yet I know I must confront him sooner or later, for my thumb tells me so."

"What does your thumb say now?" Oona asked.

Finn sucked his thumb. "He's coming," he said grimly.

Oona went to her sewing basket and drew out nine threads of different colors. She wove them into three braids that she tied around her arm, ankle, and heart. "Cheer up, my bully, you can depend on me," she said. "Just do everything I tell you."

At this Finn brightened, for he knew Oona had special connections with the fairies, and was impossibly clever as well. So he didn't protest when the first thing Oona did was dress him in baby clothes and pop him in the cradle.

Knockmany Hill jumped a few inches—and there was the hideous giant Far Rua, strutting into the yard, his third eye rolling in his head.

"I'm looking for Finn," he roared.

"He's gone to look for you," said Oona. "And woe to you if he succeeds."

"You don't know my strength," said Far Rua, and started to show her his thunderbolt-pancake.

"In that case, would you mind turning the house for me?" Oona asked sweetly. "Finn always does that when the wind blows too strong."

Far Rua put his arms around the house, picked it up, and set it down to face a different direction.

In his cradle, Finn grew damp with sweat.

"The least I can do is offer you something to eat," said Oona politely.

In came Far Rua, and Oona served him a cake—into which she had stuck the iron griddle used to cook it.

He took a big bite—*crack!*—and spat it out. "Those were the two best teeth in my head!" he growled, holding out two hairy molars.

"Why, that's the only cake my Finn eats," said Oona. "Him and the baby—they love it." She went over to the cradle and fed Finn a cake that had no griddle in it.

When Finn burped happily, Far Rua looked worried for the first time. If this was the child, what was the father like? "That baby is no joke!" he said. "How strong is he?"

"Strong enough that his favorite thing is to squeeze the water from stones," said Oona. She handed Finn a white loaf of bread that was rising by the fire.

Finn clamped his hands around it, and drops of water oozed out. When the lump of bread was small enough, he popped it into his mouth and ate it.

"Let me try," said Far Rua. Oona handed him a white stone from the fireplace. He squeezed and squeezed till he turned blue, but no water seeped out. He took a bite—and lost two more teeth.

Far Rua's knees knocked together. "I'll be going now," he said. "But before I do, let me feel what amazing teeth can chew like that."

"They're far back in his head," Oona warned.

He stuck his hand in Finn's mouth. *Snap!* When he pulled out his hand, there was nothing where his middle finger should have been. Finn gurgled happily.

Knowing that his strength was gone, Far Rua left so quickly he never discovered the tricks that had been played on him.

And neither Finn nor Oona—nor anyone else—was ever troubled by the Scottish giant again.

THE LAND OF
ETERNAL YOUTH

By the time of this Fenian legend, Finn McCool moves to the background,
and the magical land of forever-young shifts to the center.

NE MISTY SUMMER morning as Finn and
his son Usheen were hunting with companions, they
saw a beautiful maiden riding a snow-white steed. A
crown of gold was on her head, and a brown mantle of silk set with
stars of red gold fell around her. Silver shoes were on her horse's
hooves.

"From very far away I have come," she said, "and now at last I
have found you, Finn McCool."

"What do you seek from me, maiden?" said Finn.

"My name," she said, "is Niam of the Golden Hair. I am the
daughter of the king of the Land of Youth, and the love of Usheen
brings me here."

A dreamy stillness fell as the maiden spoke of her country:

> "Delightful is the land beyond all dreams,
> Fairer than your eyes have ever seen.
> There all the year the fruit is on the tree,
> And all the year the bloom is on the flower.

The feast shall not overfill, nor the chase shall tire,
Nor music cease forever through the hall;
The gold and jewels of the Land of Youth
Outshine all splendors ever dreamed by man."

To Usheen she spoke in the voice of one who never asked anything but it was granted: "Will you go with me to my father's land?"

And Usheen said: "That I will, and to the world's end," for a fairy spell had worked upon his heart.

The Fianna watched helplessly as Usheen mounted the steed with the maiden in his arms and fled down the forest glade. When the white horse reached the sea, it ran lightly over the waves, and soon the green of Erin faded. The riders passed into a golden haze in which Usheen lost all sense of where he was. Towers and palaces appeared in the mist, a hornless doe chased by a white hound, a maiden bearing a golden apple in her hand. . . .

Once in the Land of Youth, Usheen passed whole days in feasting and rejoicing and adventures. At last, after what seemed to him three weeks, full of delights of every kind, he longed to visit his native land again and see his old friends. He promised to return, so Niam gave him the steed that had brought him there. She warned him never to get off the horse—or the way back to the Land of Youth would be barred to him forever.

Usheen set forth, and found himself on the western shores of Ireland. He marveled, as he rode through the woods, at the small size of the people he saw tilling the ground. Coming to his old home, he saw it overgrown with weeds and bushes. He shouted the names of Finn and his friends, but heard only the sighing of the wind.

When he came to the eastern sea, he saw upon a hillside a crowd of men trying to roll a great boulder off their land. They all stopped their work, for he was taller and mightier than the men they knew, with sword-blue eyes and ruddy cheeks and bright hair beneath his helmet.

Usheen was filled with pity, and he stooped from his saddle to help them. He set his hand to the boulder and, with a mighty heave, got it rolling down the hill. The men raised a shout of applause, but their shouting changed into cries of terror. For Usheen's saddle slipped as he heaved the stone, and he fell headlong to the ground. The white steed vanished, and that which rose, feeble and staggering, was no youthful warrior, but a man white-bearded and withered, who moaned with feeble cries.

He gazed round with dim eyes, and at last said: "I was Usheen, the son of Finn, and I pray you tell me where he dwells."

The men gazed strangely on each other, and one asked: "Of what Finn do you speak, for there be many of that name in Erin?"

Usheen said: "Surely of Finn McCool, captain of the Fianna of Erin."

The men told him, "You are daft, old man, and have made us daft to mistake you for a youth. But we have our wits again, and we know that Finn McCool and all his generation have been dead these three hundred years."

In a minute it was as if all these years had come upon Usheen, and he was lying on the ground, turning to dust.

IRELAND

Dora Sigerson

Dora Sigerson (1866-1918) was born in Dublin to a well-known doctor father and a successful novelist mother. She became a prolific poet and wrote about the "island that sings" during a haunting time when people were streaming out of it. (Today, for the first time, with Ireland growing prosperous, more people are moving there than leaving.)

'Twas the dream of a God,
    And the mold of His hand,
That you shook 'neath His stroke,
That you trembled and broke
    To this beautiful land.

Here He loosed from His hold
    A brown tumult of wings,
Till the wind on the sea
Bore the strange melody
    Of an island that sings.

He made you all fair,
    You in purple and gold,
You in silver and green,
  Till no eye that has seen
    Without love can behold.

I have left you behind
    In the path of the past
With the white breath of flowers,
With the best of God's hours,
    I have left you at last.

IRISH BATTLE CRIES

During the days of war between feisty Irish chiefs and clans, leaders often
howled words as a weapon. Wild yells during battle inspired courage—
and scared the enemy. Some mottoes were simple—
"Look out!" and "To the victory!" Others had personality.

"Danger is sweet!" (a motto in county Westmeath)

"Short in action and mischievous in victory!"
     (the Ardrigh clan)

"We have been!" (Roscommon)

"This hand is an enemy to tyrants!" (Monaghan)

"Peace with plenty!" (Leinster)

"The uppermost!" (Westmeath and Tipperary)

"I wound and I kill!" (the Ferghail clan)

"Brave as a lion, bold as a hawk!" (Tipperary)

"First in the battle, and last in the fight!" (Clare)

"A rugged man, but excellent in battle!" (Antrim)

"Active am I in my task!" (Annally princes)

IRISH BLESSINGS

Calming down after battle, Ireland is known
for many lovely blessings and prayers.

Four corners to her bed,
Four angels at her head,
Mark, Matthew, Luke, and John;
God bless the bed that she lies on.
New moon, new moon, God bless me,
God bless this house and family.

May the road rise to meet you.
May the wind be always at your back.
May the sun shine warm upon your face.
And rains fall soft upon your fields.
And until we meet again,
May God hold you in the hollow of His hand.

Deep peace of the running wave to you.

Deep peace of the flowing air to you.

Deep peace of the quiet earth to you.

Deep peace of the shining stars to you.

Deep peace of the gentle night to you.

Moon and stars pour their healing light on you.

Deep peace of the Light of the World to you.

May the Irish hills caress you.

May her lakes and rivers bless you.

May the luck of the Irish enfold you.

May the blessings of Saint Patrick behold you.

May those who love us love us.

And those that don't love us,

May God turn their hearts.

And if He doesn't turn their hearts,

May he turn their ankles,

So we'll know them by their limping!

ALL THINGS BRIGHT AND BEAUTIFUL

Cecil Frances Alexander

Cecil Frances Alexander (1818-1895) was born in county Tyrone and
founded a school for the deaf with her sister, as well as the Girls' Friendly
Society in Londonderry. Before her marriage to the Archbishop of
Armagh, she wrote nearly 400 hymns, among which those
for children were most popular.

All things bright and beautiful,
All creatures great and small,
All things wise and wonderful,
The Lord God made them all.

Each little flower that opens,
Each little bird that sings,
He made their glowing colors,
He made their tiny wings.

The purple-headed mountain,
The river running by,
The sunset, and the morning,
That brightens up the sky;

The cold wind in the winter,
The pleasant summer sun,
The ripe fruits in the garden,
He made them every one.

He gave us eyes to see them,
And lips that we might tell,
How great is God Almighty,
Who has made all things well.

IN LOVE WITH WORDS
The Scholars

For a country its size, Ireland has produced more poets and writers than any in the world. The tradition of words goes back to the fifth through ninth centuries. While the rest of Europe was enduring the Dark Ages, Irish monks, remote from the destruction, created books the hard way—one at a time. Using pens made from feathers of geese or swans, they wrote on the skin of calves. In this fashion, book by book, they saved twelve centuries of Irish, Greek, Latin, and Hebrew literature for eternity.

THE IRISH STUDENT
AND HIS CAT

Gorgeously decorated, or illuminated, Irish manuscripts are the jewels of
libraries all over the world. While painting, monks had time to doodle their
own thoughts. This poem is believed to be by a scholar, now anonymous,
of the eighth or early ninth century.

I and Pangur Ban, my cat,
'Tis a like task we are at:
Hunting mice is his delight,
Hunting words I sit all night.

'Tis a merry thing to see
At our tasks how glad are we,
When at home we sit and find
Entertainment to our mind.

'Gainst the wall he sets his eye
Full and fierce and sharp and sly;
'Gainst the wall of knowledge I
All my little wisdom try.

85

Practice every day has made
Pangur perfect at his trade;
I get wisdom day and night,
Turning darkness into light.

So in peace our tasks we ply,
Pangur Ban, my cat, and I;
In our arts we find our bliss,
I have mine and he has his.

ODE TO WRITERS
Arthur O'Shaughnessy

Born in Dublin or Galway, Arthur O'Shaughnessy (1844-1881) wrote
poetry while working for the British Museum. This is part of a larger poem
called "Ode," about the pen being mightier than the sword.

We are the music-makers,
And we are the dreamers of dreams,
Wandering by lone sea-breakers,
And sitting by desolate streams.

World-losers and world-forsakers,
On whom the pale moon gleams:
Yet we are the movers and shakers
Of the world forever, it seems.

With wonderful deathless ditties
We build up the world's great cities,
And out of a fabulous story
We fashion an empire's glory:

One man with a dream, at pleasure,
Shall go forth and conquer a crown;
And three with a new song's measure
Can trample an empire down.

WHERE MY BOOKS GO

William Butler Yeats

Generally considered Ireland's greatest poet, William Butler Yeats was born
in 1866 in Dublin, grew up in county Sligo, spent holidays in Galway,
and published his first poem at nineteen. Champion of Irish theater
and folklore, he never stopped working to further Irish literature.
He won the 1923 Nobel Prize for literature and died in 1939.
Here he writes of the power of words to make a difference.

All the words that I utter,
And all the words that I write,
Must spread out their wings untiring,
And never rest in their flight,
Till they come where your sad, sad heart is,
And sing to you in the night,
Beyond where the waters are moving,
Storm-darken'd or starry bright.

THE MAN WHO
HAD NO STORY

In a country where words are all but worshiped, what is the worst of all fates?
To have no story to tell. This old tale considers one possible outcome.

ORY O'DONOGHUE'S WIFE was a great woman for knitting stockings, and it was Rory's job to go from town to town, selling them.

On the night before the fair in Macroom, Rory left home with his bag of stockings. Night came on before he reached the town. He saw a light in a house at the roadside, and he went in. There was no one inside but a very old man.

"Welcome, Rory O'Donoghue," said the old man.

Rory asked for lodgings for the night, and the old man said he could stay. A chair in the kitchen moved up toward the fire, and the old man told Rory to sit.

"Now," said the old man, "Rory and myself would like to have our supper."

A knife and fork jumped up from the dresser and cut down a piece of meat that was hanging from the rafters. A pot came out of the dresser, and the meat hopped into it. A bucket of water rose up, and water was poured over the meat. Potatoes rose up from a basket and went into the pot. When the meat and potatoes were boiled, plates popped out of the dresser and the knife and fork dished up the food.

After supper, the tablecloth rose up and cleared off what was left into a bucket. Rory and the old man sat at either side of the fire. Two slippers came up to Rory O'Donoghue and two others to the old man.

"Take off your shoes, and put on those slippers," said the old man. "Do you know, Rory, how I spend my nights here? I spend one-third of each night eating and drinking, one-third telling stories, and the last third sleeping. Tell a story now, Rory."

"I never told a story in my life," said Rory.

"Well, unless you tell a story, you'll have to leave," said the old man.

"I can't tell tales of any kind," said Rory. "I have not one in my head."

"Out the door with you, then."

Rory stood up and took hold of his bag of stockings. No sooner had he gone out than the door struck him a blow on the back. He went off along the road, and he hadn't gone very far when he saw the glow of a fire by the roadside. Sitting by the fire was a man roasting a piece of meat on a spit.

"Welcome, Rory O'Donoghue," said the man. "Would you

mind taking hold of this spit and turning the meat over the fire so it cooks evenly?"

No sooner had Rory taken hold of the spit than the man left him.

Then the piece of meat spoke. "Don't let my whiskers burn!" it shouted.

Rory threw the spit and the meat from him, snatched up his bag of stockings, and ran off. But the spit and the piece of meat followed him, striking Rory as hard as they could on the back. Rory caught sight of a house at the side of the road, opened the door, and ran in.

It was the same house he had visited earlier, and the old man was in bed.

"Welcome, Rory O'Donoghue," said the old man. "I'll fix up a bed for you."

"Oh, I couldn't," said Rory. "I'm a mess!"

"What happened to you since you left here?" asked the old man.

"Oh, the abuse I got from a piece of meat that a man was roasting by the roadside," said Rory. "He asked me to turn the meat on the spit for a while, and 'twasn't long till the meat screamed at me not to burn its whiskers. I threw it from me, but it followed me, giving me such blows that I'm all cut and bruised."

"Ah, Rory," said the old man. "If you'd had a story like that to tell me before, when I asked you, you wouldn't have had to go out

93

at all. From now on, whenever anybody asks you to tell a story, tell that one, and you will be the man who has a story to tell."

Rory went to bed and fell asleep. When he awoke in the morning, he found himself on the roadside, with his bag of stockings under his head, and not a trace of a house or a dwelling anywhere around him.

FIELDS AND FARMS
The Land

Ireland's landscape is all green, all the time.
The endless green of fields and farms dotted with blue lakes like
jewels, swampy sections (bogs), narrow roads where cars must
yield to sheep (which still outnumber the people), boundaries of
stone walls, occasional fabulous castles. . . . It is simply one of
the most beautiful places on earth—unspoiled compared to other,
more industrialized countries. A calm, stable land—
no earthquake has ever been recorded here.

THE WIND THAT SHAKES THE BARLEY

Katherine Tynan

Throughout miles of silent countryside, sometimes the only sound is
the wind rustling the leaves of barley, as well as Ireland's other crops
and its stunning wildflowers.

There's music in my heart all day,
I hear it late and early,
It comes from fields are far away,
The wind that shakes the barley.

Above the uplands drenched with dew
The sky hangs soft and pearly,
An emerald world is listening to
The wind that shakes the barley.

Above the bluest mountain crest
The lark is singing rarely,
It rocks the singer into rest,
The wind that shakes the barley.

Oh, still through summers and through springs
It calls me late and early,
Come home, come home, come home, it sings,
The wind that shakes the barley.

DONALD O'NEARY AND HIS NEIGHBORS

This variation on the trickster-hero tale takes place in the Irish countryside.
Two rich, but dumb, farmers are about to meet their match:
a poor, but crafty, neighbor.

NCE UPON A TIME, a poor man named Donald O'Neary lived on a tiny strip of land in between two large, thriving farms. He barely had a roof over his head, and his strip of grass was hardly enough to keep his one skinny cow, Daisy, alive.

The two rich farmers were named Hudden and Dudden, and they owned goats and chickens and sheep and cattle and plenty of land.

You might think that Hudden and Dudden would be happy with all that they had, but they were greedy men. Each night they lay in bed thinking of ways to take away poor Donald O'Neary's strip of land.

At last they decided to poison Daisy, for they thought that without his cow, Donald would move away.

When Donald saw Daisy had died, he said, "She's better off now. She was always starving." But he began to wonder if he could get any good out of his cow's death. . . .

The next market day he carried Daisy's hide to the village. Every penny he had was jingling in his pocket—there were only a few. Just before he reached the village, he cut a few slits in the hide, and in each slit he placed a penny.

Donald marched into the finest inn and hung the hide on the wall. "Bring me your best food," he called to the innkeeper. "And don't fear I won't be paying you." Donald whacked Daisy's hide with his stick and out popped a penny. "Just look here, this hide of mine gives me all the money I want."

You can imagine the innkeeper's surprise. "So, what'll you take for it?" he asked.

"It's not for sale! Hasn't it kept me and mine for years?" Donald whacked again, and out popped a second penny.

The innkeeper begged and pleaded until at last Donald sold him the hide. That night he walked to his neighbor Hudden's house.

"Evening, Hudden. I'd like to borrow your scale to weigh my gold."

Hudden couldn't believe his ears. Since when did Donald O'Neary have gold? But he lent the scale to Donald, though first he smeared it with butter.

Back home Donald weighed the gold the innkeeper had paid him. When he returned the scale, a piece of gold had stuck to the butter.

If Hudden was shocked before, now he was delighted. He ran to Dudden's place and told him the whole tale. "He must have sacks full of gold!"

The pair decided to pay Donald a visit.

"Evening, Hudden. Evening, Dudden," Donald said. "Ah, you did a fine deed in destroying my Daisy. Hides are worth their weight in gold these days, you know."

The very next day, Hudden and Dudden got up before dawn, killed a dozen of their cows, and took their hides to market. "Hides to sell!" they called. "Worth their weight in gold!"

Everyone seemed to think they were crazy.

And when the innkeeper heard them, he accused them of cheating him the day before. He had whacked Daisy's hide a great many times, and not a single penny popped out. He was furious, for he had paid dearly for that hide. Now the innkeeper chased Hudden and Dudden, yelling, "Catch those thieves!"

Hudden and Dudden took off, all the dogs of the town at their heels. When they came to Donald O'Neary's house, Hudden cried, "Let's get him!" They grabbed Donald and popped him inside an empty flour sack. They knotted the sack up tight and started off for the Brown Lake of the Bog. It was time to get rid of Donald once and for all.

The Bog was far, and Hudden and Dudden were weary, so

when they came to an inn by the roadside, they stopped to rest. They dumped Donald by the door as if he were a sack of potatoes. "Be quiet," they warned him.

Soon Hudden and Dudden were inside laughing and singing away.

Donald heard a farmer driving his cattle past his sack and he cried out, "I won't have her, I tell you! I simply won't!"

"And who won't you have?" the farmer asked the talking sack.

"They're forcing me to marry the king's daughter. Imagine! So what if she's beautiful, covered in jewels from head to toe? I don't love her. Please help me escape."

The farmer let Donald out and took his place. He did not mind the idea of marrying the king's daughter. Indeed, he offered Donald his herd of cattle in exchange.

When Hudden and Dudden came out, they dragged the sack the rest of the way to the lake, pitched it in, and went home all light-hearted.

No sooner had they arrived than they saw Donald O'Neary surrounded by a herd of fine cows. Hudden stared. Dudden gasped.

Donald grinned. He waved and said, "Thank you again! You knew Brown Lake leads to a land full of fat cattle. It was a struggle just to bring up this skinny bunch!"

Hudden and Dudden ran right back to the lake and jumped in.

But they never came back. Maybe they grew too fat, like the cattle.

As for Donald O'Neary, he happily worked the land and took good care of his cattle all the rest of his days.

THE LAKE ISLE
OF INNISFREE

William Butler Yeats

Innisfree is a real place—a small wooded island rising out of Lough Gill
("Lake of Brightness") in county Sligo. Influenced by Henry David
Thoreau's *Walden*, Yeats dreamed of escaping from gray cities to a
simpler life in a cottage he would shape out of clay and wattles,
or interwoven branches of trees.

I will arise and go now, and go to Innisfree,
And a small cabin build there, of clay and wattles made:
Nine bean-rows will I have there, a hive for the honeybee,
And live alone in the bee-loud glade.

And I shall have some peace there, for peace comes
    dropping slow,
Dropping from the veils of the morning to where the
    cricket sings;
There midnight's all a glimmer, and noon a purple glow,
And evening full of the linnet's wings.

I will arise and go now, for always night and day
I hear lake water lapping with low sounds by the shore;
While I stand on the roadway, or on the pavements gray,
I hear it in the deep heart's core.

MY LAND
Thomas Davis

Thomas Davis was born in Cork in 1814 and died in Dublin in 1845. He
founded the Young Ireland Party and, in the last three years of his short life,
wrote poetry intended to make the Irish more aware of their heritage.

She is a rich and rare land,
Oh, she's a fresh and fair land;
She is a dear and rare land,
This native land of mine.

No men than hers are braver,
Her women's hearts ne'er waver;
I'd freely die to save her,
And think my lot divine.

My Land

She's not a dull or cold land,
No, she's a warm and bold land,
Oh, she's a true and old land,
This native land of mine.

Could beauty ever guard her,
And virtue still reward her,
No foe would cross her border—
No friend within it pine.

Oh, she's a fresh and fair land,
Oh, she's a true and rare land;
Yes, she's a rare and fair land,
This native land of mine.

ENCHANTMENT
The Fairies

Most of this book would like to squeeze into this chapter: fairy lore lives and breathes throughout Ireland. Generally, fairies are a few inches high, almost transparent. They are rumored to be very beautiful, with long yellow hair and bodies as delicate as dewdrops. They drink flower nectar, and they love music, often luring mortals into an eternal dance with their piping and singing. Their greatest reward is the famous pot of gold. Bad fairies are thought to bewitch children, substitute ugly fairy babies (known as changelings) for human infants, and kill off cattle. Most fairies, when treated with the proper respect, seem to be kindly, if sensitive, and inclined to play pranks. But fairies can assume any form and any mood—and that is where the trickery, or magic, triumphs.

THE FAIRIES IN NEW ROSS

Fairies delight in making a dramatic entrance.
Whisper this poem in your best fairy voice.

When moonlight
Near midnight
Tips the rock and waving wood;

When moonlight
Near midnight
Silvers o'er the sleeping flood;

When yew-tops
With dew-drops
Sparkle o'er deserted graves;

'Tis then we fly
Through welkin* high,
Then we sail o'er yellow waves.

*The sky

THE FAIRIES
William Allingham

This eerie song, a child's-eye view of fairies, is probably the most commonly
reprinted Irish poem, and the most popular one by William Allingham
(1824-1889). He grew up in county Donegal, and worked as a bank clerk,
magazine editor, and prolific writer. Each night at twilight, he was in the
habit of strolling the streets of Ballyshannon listening to women singing
old ballads by their cottage doors.

Up the airy mountain,
Down the rushy glen,
We daren't go a-hunting
For fear of little men;
Wee folk, good folk,
Trooping all together;
Green jacket, red cap,
And white owl's feather!

Down along the rocky shore
Some make their home,
They live on crispy pancakes
Of yellow tide-foam;
Some in the reeds
Of the black mountain lake,

With frogs for their watchdogs,
All night awake.

High on the hill-top
The old King sits;
He is now so old and gray
He's nigh lost his wits.
With a bridge of white mist
Columbkill he crosses,
On his stately journeys
From Slieveleague to Rosses;
Or going up with music
On cold starry nights
To sup with the Queen
Of the gay Northern Lights.

They stole little Bridget
For seven years long;
When she came down again
Her friends were all gone.
They took her lightly back,
Between the night and morrow.
They thought that she was fast asleep,
But she was dead with sorrow.

They have kept her ever since
Deep within the lake,
On a bed of flag-leaves,
Watching till she wake.

By the craggy hillside,
Through the mosses bare,
They have planted thorn-trees
For pleasure here and there.
If any man so daring
As dig them up in spite,
He shall find their sharpest thorns
In his bed at night.

Up the airy mountain,
Down the rushy glen,
We daren't go a-hunting
For fear of little men;
Wee folk, good folk,
Trooping all together;
Green jacket, red cap,
And white owl's feather!

FAIR, BROWN, AND TREMBLING

Every culture, it seems, has its own Cinderella story, and here is Ireland's.

NCE IN BALLYSHANNON there were three sisters whose names were Fair, Brown, and Trembling.

Fair and Brown got new dresses and went to church every Sunday. They would not let Trembling out of the house at all. She was so much more beautiful that they lived in dread she might marry first. She wore rags and stayed home to do all the work.

One Sunday morning, after the other two had gone to church, the old henwife came into the kitchen to Trembling and asked why she wasn't at church.

"I have no clothes good enough," said Trembling. "Besides, my sisters would kill me for leaving the house."

"I'll give you a finer dress than either of them has ever seen," said the henwife. "What would you like?"

"A dress as white as snow, please, and green shoes for my feet," said Trembling.

The henwife put on her cloak of darkness, clipped a piece from the rags the young woman had on, and asked for the whitest robes in the world and a pair of green shoes.

When Trembling was dressed and ready, the henwife said, "I have a honey-bird here to sit on your right shoulder, and a honey-flower to put on your left. At the door stands a milk-white mare."

As Trembling sat on the golden saddle, the henwife said, "You must not go inside the church door, and the minute the people rise up at the end of Mass, ride home as fast as the mare will carry you."

When Trembling got to the church, everyone who glimpsed her wanted to know who she was. But she was gone before any man could come near. All the way home, she overtook the wind before her, and outstripped the wind behind.

In the kitchen, she found that the henwife had dinner all ready. She put off the white robes, and had on her old rags in a twinkling.

When the two sisters came home, they couldn't stop talking about the grand lady at church. "There wasn't a man, from the king to the beggar, who wasn't trying to find out who she was."

The sisters would give no peace till they had two dresses like the robes of the strange lady, though honey-birds and honey-flowers were not to be found.

Next Sunday they went to church and left the youngest at home to cook dinner.

After they had gone, Trembling asked this of the henwife: "The

finest black satin dress that can be found, red shoes for my feet, and a mare so black and glossy that I can see myself in her body."

The henwife put on her cloak of darkness and asked for the robes and the mare, then put the honey-bird on the girl's right shoulder and the honey-flower on her left.

When Trembling was sitting in the silver saddle, the henwife again warned her not to go inside the door and to rush away as soon as Mass ended.

The people at church were more astonished than ever, but the moment they rose, she was in the silver saddle and home before a man could stop her.

The henwife had dinner all ready, and Trembling had on her old clothes before her sisters got home.

"We saw the grand strange lady again!" the sisters exclaimed. "And all at church, from high to low, had their mouths open, and no man was looking at us."

The two sisters gave no one any peace till they got dresses as nearly like the strange lady's robes as they could find. Once again, they went to church on Sunday, leaving Trembling at work.

The henwife came to the kitchen and said, "Well, my dear. . . ?"

"I would go—if I had a dress red as a rose from the waist down,

and white as snow from the waist up; a cape of green on my shoulders; and a hat with a feather in it; and shoes with the toes red, the middle white, and the backs and heels green."

The henwife put on her cloak, wished for all these things, and had them. She put the bird on Trembling's right shoulder and the flower on her left, and clipped a few hairs from her locks. The most beautiful golden hair flowed down over the girl's shoulders.

She mounted a white mare on a saddle of gold.

All the princes of the world came to church that Sunday, each hoping to meet her. Among them was the son of the King of Emania in Ulster.

After Mass, Trembling was in the saddle and sweeping away ahead of the wind.

But the prince of Emania was at her side and, seizing her by the foot, never let go till he pulled the shoe right off. She came home as fast as the mare could carry her, sure that the henwife would kill her for losing the shoe.

But the henwife seemed almost pleased. The sisters arrived and never stopped talking about "the most beautiful woman ever seen by man in Erin."

All the princes of the world began to search for the mystery-woman. The prince of Emania traveled north, south, east, and west. He carried the shoe, and when young women saw it, they had great

hopes, for it was normal size, though no one could say of what material. One thought it would fit her if she cut a little from her big toe;
and another, with a short foot, put something in the tip of her stocking. But they only spoiled their feet, and were curing them for
months afterward.

On the day the prince came to see Fair and Brown, the two sisters put Trembling in a closet and locked the door.

But though they tried and tried, the shoe would fit neither of
them.

"Is there any other young woman in the house?" asked the prince.

"There is," said Trembling, speaking up in the closet. "I'm here."

The shoe was given to Trembling, and it fit exactly.

"Who are you?" the prince asked in wonder.

"Oh! We only keep her to put out the ashes," said the sisters.

Nothing would do but that Trembling had to fetch the henwife. The old woman put on the cloak of darkness and transformed
the younger with each of the three dresses.

Everyone was satisfied, and knew that she was the right
woman.

Other princes arrived, telling the prince of Emania, "You'll
have to fight for her before we let her go with you."

The son of the king of Lochlin stepped forth, and a terrible
struggle it was. They fought for nine hours, and then the Lochlin

prince gave up. Next day the son of the king of Spain fought six hours, and yielded his claim. The third day the son of the king of Greece fought four hours, and stopped. On the fifth day all the Erin princes said they would not fight with a man of their own land and would yield to the prince of Emania.

The wedding lasted for a year and a day.

After a son was born, Trembling sent for her eldest sister, Fair, to help out.

One day, when her husband was out hunting, the two sisters went for a walk. When they came to the seaside, the eldest pushed the youngest sister in. A great whale came and swallowed her.

The eldest sister came home and pretended to be Trembling, for indeed they looked a bit alike.

"My sister Fair has gone home, now that I am well," she told the prince.

The prince was in doubt. That night he put his sword between them, and said, "If you are my wife, this sword will get warm. If not, it will stay cold."

In the morning, the sword was as cold as when he put it there.

It so happened that when the two sisters were at the shore, a young cowherd was minding his cattle. He saw all that took place, and the next day, when the tide came in, he saw the whale swim up and throw Trembling out on the sand.

"Tell the master," she said to the cowherd, "that the whale will swallow me with the next tide. The whale will cast me out three times—I'm under its enchantment. Unless my husband saves me before the fourth time, I shall be lost. He must shoot the whale with a silver bullet in a reddish-brown spot under the breast fin."

But when the cowherd got home, the eldest sister gave him a potion of forgetfulness, and he did not tell.

Next day he went again to the sea. The whale came and cast Trembling on shore. She told the boy, "Don't forget what I said, and if she gives you a drink, don't take it."

As soon as the cowherd came home, the eldest sister offered him a drink. He refused and told all to the master.

The third day the prince went to the sea with his gun and a silver bullet in it. He was not there long before the whale threw Trembling upon the beach. She had no power to speak to her husband till he had killed the whale. The whale went back out to sea, turned over, and showed the reddish-brown spot. The prince had but the one chance, but he took it and hit the spot, and the whale turned the sea red with blood.

The prince had Fair put out to the sea in a barrel, with enough food for seven years.

Trembling and the prince had a second child, a daughter. They sent the cowherd to school, and in time he and Trembling's daughter fell in love and were married.

The prince and Trembling lived on to have fourteen children in all, happy till the two died of old age.

THE STOLEN CHILD

William Butler Yeats

This dreamy, unearthly poem, in the voice of the fairies, is one of Yeats's
most popular. It plays on the superstition that fairies were in the habit of steal-
ing children—and that they could make this look very attractive. All the places
mentioned are in county Sligo, where the poet spent much of his childhood.

Where dips the rocky highland
Of Sleuth Wood in the lake,
There lies a leafy island
Where flapping herons wake
The drowsy water rats;
There we've hid our fairy vats,
Full of berries,
And of the reddest stolen cherries.
Come away, O human child!
To the waters and the wild
With a fairy, hand in hand,
For the world's more full of weeping
*   than you can understand.*

Where the wave of moonlight glosses
The dim gray sands with light,
Far off by furthest Rosses

We foot it all the night,
Weaving olden dances,
Mingling hands and mingling glances
Till the moon has taken flight;
To and fro we leap
And chase the frothy bubbles,
While the world is full of troubles
And is anxious in its sleep.

Come away, O human child!
To the waters and the wild
With a fairy, hand in hand,
For the world's more full of weeping
  than you can understand.

Where the wandering water gushes
From the hills above Glen-Car,
In the pools among the rushes
That scarce could bathe a star,
We seek for slumbering trout
And whispering in their ears
Give them unquiet dreams;
Leaning softly out
From ferns that drop their tears
Over the young streams.

Come away, O human child!
To the waters and the wild
With a fairy, hand in hand,
For the world's more full of weeping
    than you can understand.

Away with us he's going,
The solemn-eyed:
He'll hear no more lowing
Of the calves on the warm hillside;
Or the kettle on the hob
Sing peace into his breast,
Or see the brown mice bob
Round and round the oatmeal-chest
For here he comes, the human child,
To the waters and the wild
With a fairy, hand in hand,
From a world more full of weeping
    than he can understand.

TO CURE A CHILD UNDER
A FAIRY SPELL

MAKE A GOOD FIRE and throw into it a handful of herbs used by fairies. When a great smoke rises, carry the child three times around the fire, reciting a charm against evil. Keep the doors tightly closed, or the fairies will come in to see what you are doing. Continue reciting until the child sneezes three times, and you will know the child has been released from fairy spells forevermore.

THE STAR-CHILD

Adapted from the fairy tale by Oscar Wilde

Oscar Wilde, born in Dublin in 1854, had distinguished parents
(a famous eye surgeon and Lady Wilde, a passionate Irish patriot and
writer). He grew up to become a colorful writer of plays, poetry,
and much else, and died in 1900.

 NCE UPON A TIME, two poor woodcutters were making their way home through a great pine forest. The snow lay thick upon the ground, and the frost kept snapping the twigs on either side of them.

Suddenly there fell from heaven a very bright star. As the woodcutters watched in wonder, it seemed to sink behind a clump of willows no more than a stone's throw away.

"A pot of gold for whoever finds it!" they cried, and they set off running.

They came to something lying on the white snow—a cloak of golden tissue, curiously decorated with stars, and wrapped in many folds.

They pulled apart the cloak that they might divide the pieces of gold. But, alas! no gold was in it, nor treasure of any kind, but only a little child asleep.

One of them said to the other: "Let us go our way, seeing that we are poor men and have hungry children of our own."

But his companion answered, "It's an evil thing to leave the child to perish here in the snow, and though I have many mouths to feed, I will bring it home with me."

So the Star-Child was brought up with the children of the woodcutter, and sat at the same table with them, and was their playmate. The woodcutter took the curious cloak of gold and placed it in a great chest.

Every year the child became more beautiful to look at, so that the villagers were filled with wonder. His curls were like the rings of the daffodil, his lips like the petals of a red flower, and his eyes were like violets by a river of pure water.

Yet for all his beauty, he grew up to be cruel and selfish. He called other children his servants while saying he was noble, being sprung from a Star. He hurt animals, and he mocked the ill and weak. In summer, he would lie by the well in the priest's orchard and look down at his own face and laugh with pleasure.

And companions would follow him in all things, for besides being fair, he was fleet of foot and could dance, pipe, and make music.

Now there passed one day through the village a poor beggar-woman. Under a chestnut tree she sat down to rest her feet, bleeding from the rough road.

When the Star-Child saw her, he came near and threw stones at her.

The woodcutter, cutting logs nearby, ran up and spoke to the Star-Child harshly.

The Star-Child stamped his foot. "I am no son of yours to do your bidding."

"You speak the truth," answered the woodcutter, "yet did I show pity when I found you in the forest."

When the woman heard this she gave a cry and looked like she might faint. "Did you say that the child was found in the forest? And was it not ten years from this day?"

The woodcutter answered, "Yes to both of your questions."

"Was not round him a cloak of gold tissue embroidered with stars?" she cried.

The woodcutter fetched the cloak from the chest, and showed it to her.

The woman wept for joy, and turned to the boy. "I am your mother," she said.

The Star-Child laughed scornfully. "I am no son of an ugly beggar in rags."

"You are indeed my little son who I delivered in the forest," she cried, holding out her arms to him. "The robbers stole you from me, and left you to die. Over the whole world have I wandered in search of you. Come with me, for I have need of your love."

But the Star-Child shut the doors of his heart. "If in truth you are my mother, it were better you stayed away, and not bring me shame, seeing that I thought I was the child of some Star and not a beggar's child. Let me see you no more."

"Alas! my son," she cried, "will you not kiss me before I go? For I have suffered much to find you."

"I would rather kiss the snake or the toad," said the Star-Child, and ran off to be with his playmates.

But when they saw him coming, they mocked him. "Why, you are as foul as the toad, and as loathsome as the snake. We will not suffer you to play with us."

The Star-Child went to the well of water and looked into it, and lo! his face was a toad's, his body scaled like a snake's. He flung himself down on the grass and wept: "I have been cruel to my mother, and as a punishment this evil has been sent to me."

He ran into the forest and called out to his mother, but there was no answer. When the sun set he slept on a bed of leaves, and in the morning he ate some bitter berries from the trees.

On his way through the great woods, he asked help of everyone he met.

He said to the Mole, "You can go beneath the earth. Tell me, is my mother there?"

The Mole answered, "You were the one who blinded my eyes. How should I know?"

He said to the Linnet, "You can fly over the tops of trees and see the whole world. Tell me, can you see my mother?"

The Linnet answered, "You clipped my wings for your pleasure. How should I fly?"

To the lonely little Squirrel who lived in the fir tree, he said, "Where is my mother?"

The Squirrel answered, "You have slain mine. Do you seek to slay yours also?"

The Star-Child wept and prayed forgiveness of God's things, and walked on. On the third day he came to the other side of the forest and went down into the plain.

When he passed through villages children threw stones at him.

No one would let him sleep in the barns lest he bring mildew on the stored corn, so foul was he to look at.

For three years he wandered. One evening he came to the gate of a strong-walled city. Soldiers laughed at his questions and pricked him with their spears.

"Let us sell the foul thing for a slave," said one of them, "and divide up the money among us."

A man passing by called out, "I will buy him from you." When he had paid the price, he took the Star-Child by the hand and led him into the city.

Soon the Star-Child found himself in a dungeon lit by a lantern of horn.

The old man gave him moldy bread and some salty water in a cup, then went out, locking the door behind him with an iron chain.

In the morning the old man, who was indeed an evil magician, came in to him and said, "In a wood near the gate of this city there are three pieces of gold. One is white, another is yellow, and the third one is red. Today you shall bring me the piece of white gold, and if you fail I will beat you with a hundred lashes."

The Star-Child went out into the street, and walked to the wood of which the magician had spoken. This wood seemed full of singing birds and sweet-scented flowers, but wherever he stepped harsh briars and thorns shot up from the ground and tripped him.

Evil nettles stung him, and the thistle pierced him with her daggers. And he could not find anywhere the piece of white gold, though he sought from morn to noon, and from noon to sunset. At sunset he set his face toward home, weeping bitterly.

At the edge of the wood, he heard a cry as of someone in pain. He ran back to a thicket and saw a little Hare caught in a trap that some hunter had set for it.

The Star-Child took pity on it, and released it, saying, "I am myself but a slave, yet may I give you your freedom."

"What shall I give you in return?" the Hare answered.

The Star-Child explained his search for the piece of white gold. Then he followed the Hare, and lo! in the opening of a great oak tree he found it. Filled with joy, he said to the Hare, "The service that I did for you has been repaid a hundredfold."

"As you dealt with me," answered the Hare, "so I did deal with you." It ran away swiftly, and the Star-Child walked toward the city.

At the gate there was seated a leper, his eyes gleaming like red coals. When he saw the Star-Child coming, he struck upon a wooden bowl, clattered his bell, and called, "Give me money, or I will die of hunger."

"Alas," said the Star-Child, "I have but one piece of money."

But the leper begged, until the Star-Child had pity and gave him the white gold.

That night the magician, finding the Star-Child without the white gold, fell upon him and beat him.

In the morning, he returned to the dungeon and said, "If today you fail to bring me the piece of yellow gold, I will continue to keep you as my slave, and give you three hundred lashes."

So the Star-Child went to the wood and searched for the piece of yellow gold. At sunset he sat down and began to weep, and there came to him the little Hare.

"Follow me," cried the Hare, and it ran through the wood till it came to a pool of water. At the bottom of the pool was the yellow gold.

The Star-Child hurried back to the city. But the leper ran to meet him, crying, "Give me money or I shall die of hunger." The leper pleaded so much that the Star-Child had pity on him, and gave him the gold.

That night the magician beat him and cast him again into the dungeon.

The next morning the magician said, "If today you bring me the piece of red gold I will set you free, but if not I will surely slay you."

All day long the Star-Child searched for the red gold, weeping.

And the Hare said to him, "The red gold you seek is in the cavern behind you. Weep no more but be glad."

"This is the third time you have saved me," said the Star-Child.

"You had pity on me first," said the Hare, and it ran away swiftly.

The Star-Child rushed to the city, but the leper blocked his way, standing in the center of the road. "Give me the piece of red money, or I must die," he cried.

The Star-Child had pity on him once again, saying, "Your need is greater than mine." Yet his heart was heavy, for he knew what evil fate awaited him.

But as he passed through the gate of the city, the guards bowed down before him, saying, "How beautiful is our lord!" Such a noisy crowd gathered around that the Star-Child lost his way, and found himself at last in a great square, before the palace of a king.

The palace doors opened, and the priests and officers of the city ran to meet him. "It was prophesied," they told him, "that on this day should come he who was to rule over us. Take this crown and this scepter, and be in his justice and mercy our king."

A guard held up his shield of shiny armor. The Star-Child looked, and lo! his face was even as it had been, and his beauty had come back to him, and he saw in his eyes that which he had not seen before.

But to those kneeling before him, he said, "I am not worthy, for I have denied the mother who bore me, nor may I rest till I have found her." He turned to leave the city, and lo! among the crowd that pressed round the soldiers, he saw the beggar-woman who was his mother, and at her side stood the leper who had sat by the road.

He ran over, and kneeling down he kissed the wounds on his mother's feet, and wet them with his tears, sobbing, "Mother, I denied you in the hour of my pride. Accept me in the hour of my humility."

But the beggar-woman answered him not a word.

The Star-Child clasped the white feet of the leper, and said, "Three times did I give you mercy. Bid my mother speak to me once."

But the leper answered him not a word.

He sobbed again, "Mother, give me forgiveness, let me go back to the forest."

And the beggar-woman put her hand on his head, and said to him, "Rise."

And the leper put his hand on his head, and said to him, "Rise," also.

And he rose up and looked and lo! they were a king and a queen.

"This is your father who you have aided," the queen said.

"And your mother, whose feet you have washed with your tears," the king said.

And they fell on his neck and kissed him, brought him into the palace, and set the crown upon his head. Over the city he ruled, with much justice and mercy to all. Nor would he allow any to be cruel to bird or beast, but taught love and kindness and charity, and there was peace and plenty in the land.

WHO MAKES THE FAIRIES' SHOES?
The Leprechauns

Actually, there are too many types of Irish fairies to include them all in this book. The kind everyone knows is the leprechaun. According to legend, a leprechaun is usually unfriendly (even crabby) and cleverer than you. He lives alone and passes the time making shoes. Fairy shoes wear out quickly from all their dancing, so there is plenty of work. He looks like a small old man, with a face like a dried apple. Most importantly, he owns a hidden pot of gold—about which there are certain rules.

PATRICK O'DONNELL
AND THE
LEPRECHAUN

Finding a leprechaun can be like winning the lottery . . . if you remember to never, ever take your eyes off him.

 ATRICK O'DONNELL was walking home one night from the Donegal county fair. As he came over a hill, he heard a shrill little scream out in the swamp.

It sounded like a bird, but he had never heard a bird like this. So he made his way out into the bog, taking care not to sink in the thick mud. Thornbushes snatched at his clothes and hands, but he kept going, that shrill little cry urging him onward.

Finally he reached the middle of the bog, and blinked his eyes in surprise. The moon overhead was bright and full, so he could see quite well. And there, caught by his pants on a long black thorn, was a little fairy man!

"Poor wee thing," said Patrick, bending down. Then he caught sight of a tiny cobbler's bench under the thornbush. "Why, you're a leprechaun!"

The little man swung at him with both fists, but he was firmly trapped on the thorn. "Just get me down! And be careful, these are new pants!"

Well, Patrick O'Donnell was no fool, and he remembered the old stories very well. Leprechauns always had magical pots of gold that never emptied themselves hidden nearby. And if you could catch one, and you never took your eyes off him, he'd have to do anything you said. So if he asked for this leprechaun's pot of gold, the leprechaun would have to show him where it was hidden.

"I'll help you," he said, gently taking the little man off the thorn. "But I'm not letting you out of my sight. I want your pot of gold, so I can feed my family!"

The leprechaun shook his head. "You'd better go take care of your father's animals," he said, pointing past Patrick. "Look, the fence has broken and the cattle are getting loose."

Patrick almost turned to look, but then he saw through the trick. He had to keep his eyes on the leprechaun, or it would escape.

"Oh, very well," the leprechaun sighed. "Put me down. I have a big pot of gold in the field over there. I'll show you."

As the moon rose across the sky, Patrick made his way deeper into the swamp, careful not to look away from the leprechaun. They came to a certain black thornbush. "My gold is hidden under that bush," the leprechaun told him with a scowl.

Patrick looked around the swamp, at the thousands of black thornbushes. In the moonlight they all looked the same. "Are you sure this is the right one?" he asked.

"As sure as I am that I'm the one who mends all fairies' shoes after they're worn out from dancing! Just dig under that bush, if you must, and you'll find your pot of gold."

But poor Patrick didn't have so much as a sharp stick to dig with. "If I go home for a shovel, I'll never be able to find my way back to this bush!" he cried.

"Not my fault," the leprechaun said. "You wanted to know where it was, and I've shown you. Getting it home is your problem."

Patrick thought and thought, and finally he had an idea. "I'll tie my red scarf to the bush! Even in the darkness, I'll be able to see it, and find my way back."

The leprechaun began to laugh. "That's your solution?" he asked. "Very well, then, I'll be on my way now!"

Now that the magical pot was almost his, Patrick let go of the little man, who vanished like a shooting star into the night. Patrick tied his scarf tightly around the bush.

It took him the rest of the night to make his way out of the swamp, go home for a shovel, and return. He chuckled all the way, saying, "I'll be rich for the rest of my life, and I'll never have to work again!"

The sun was glowing orange by the time Patrick stumbled back into the swamp, still chuckling. He was halfway across the huge field before he noticed that every single thornbush had a red scarf tied around it, and each scarf was exactly the same as his!

"That wicked leprechaun!" Patrick cried, shaking his head. "If I live to be a hundred, I'll never be able to dig up every thornbush in this field!"

So with a heavy heart, he threw his shovel down and stomped home. And until he was an old man, he told his children, and their children, and their children after that, about the big field of thorn-bushes, and the magical pot of gold.

THE LEPRECHAUN
William Allingham

Lay your ear close to the hill—
Do you not catch the tiny clamor,
Busy click of an elfin hammer,
Voice of the leprechaun singing shrill,
As he busily plies his trade?

I caught him at work one day, myself,
In the castle-ditch, where foxglove grows;
A wrinkled, wizened, and bearded elf,
Spectacles stuck on his pointed nose,
Silver buckles to his hose,
Leather apron, shoe in his lap—
"Tip-rap, tip-tap,
Tick-tack-too,
(A grasshopper on my cap!
Away the moth flew!)
Buskins for a fairy prince,
Brogues for his son—
Pay me well, pay me well
When the job is done!"

The rogue was mine, beyond a doubt.

I stared at him; he stared at me;

"Servant, sir! Humph!" says he,

And pulled a snuffbox out.

He took a long pinch, looked better pleased,

The queer little leprechaun;

Offered the box with a whimsical grace—

Poof! he flung the dust in my face,

And while I sneezed,

Was gone!

THE LEPRECHAUN

Robert Dwyer Joyce

Robert Dwyer Joyce (1830-1883) was born in Limerick, became a professor
of English literature, and wrote numerous books. In danger of arrest for his
political views, he left Ireland and worked as a doctor in Boston.

In a shady nook one moonlit night,
A leprechaun I spied
In scarlet coat and cap of green,
A cruiskeen* by his side.

'Twas tick, tack, tick, his hammer went,
Upon a weenie shoe,
And I laughed to think of a purse of gold,
But the fairy was laughing, too.

With tip-toe step and beating heart,
Quite softly I drew nigh.
There was mischief in his merry face,
A twinkle in his eye;

*Flask

The Leprechaun

He hammered and sang with tiny voice,
And sipped the mountain dew;
Oh! I laughed to think he was caught at last,
But the fairy was laughing, too.

As quick as thought I grasped the elf,
"Your fairy purse," I cried,
"My purse?" said he, "'tis in her hand,
That lady by your side."

I turned to look, the elf was off,
And what was I to do?
Oh! I laughed to think what a fool I'd been,
And the fairy was laughing, too.

PEOPLE NEVER STOP TALKING
The Blarney

"It is a lovely country, but very melancholy, except that people never stop talking."

—Virginia Woolf,
English writer

WHAT IT IS,
HOW TO DO IT, AND
THE BLARNEY STONE

NCE THERE was a real Lord of Blarney. In the early 1600s, while taking orders from England's Queen Elizabeth I, he had a way of seeming to agree while putting her off with his gentle, witty talking.

One day she exclaimed, "This is all Blarney—what he says he never means!"

And ever since, *blarney* has referred to an Irish way of speaking sweetly and convincingly—a real way with words, if you like it. Double-talk, if you don't.

Set in the wall of Blarney Castle tower, built in 1446 in county Cork, is a hunk of limestone. The legend has spread that kissing this Blarney Stone brings the kisser the gift of blarney. Kissers have to lie on their back and bend backward, holding iron bars for support, with nothing but empty air underneath them. If this proves too challenging, you can try learning how to blarney at home.

To blarney, it helps to be born with the "gift of the gab." You can also learn how to say flattering things in ways that people like. You could also start out with nonsense like this:

Rum fum boodle boo,
Ripple dipple nitty dob;
Dumdoo doodle coo,
Raffle taffle chittiboo!

LIMERICKS

Limerick is a county in Ireland. It is also a humorous poem of five lines, with a rhyme scheme of a-a-b-b-a. Most fun is making up your own. The name might come from the chorus of an eighteenth-century Irish soldiers' song, "Will You Come Up to Limerick?"

There once were two cats of Kilkenny;
Each thought there was one cat too many.
    So they fought and they fit,
    And they scratched and they bit,
Till instead of two cats there weren't any.

There was a young maid of Tralee
Whose knowledge of French was "Oui, oui."
    When they said, "Parlez vous?"
    She replied, "Same to you."
She was famed for her bright repartee!

An Irishman owned an old barge,
But his nose was exceedingly large.
    But in fishing by night
    It supported a light—
Which helped the old man with his charge.

A young lass from near Killenaule
Wore a newspaper dress to a ball.
  The dress it caught fire,
  Burned up the entire—
Front page, sporting section, and all!

A bishop residing in Meath
Sat down on his set of false teeth;
  Said he, with a start,
  "O Lord, bless my heart,
I've bitten myself underneath!"

A shy girl was Molly McClure,
With a mind that was holy and pure,
  She fainted away
  In a delicate way
If anyone mentioned manure.

There was an old man of Kilkenny
Who ate sixty-five eggs for a penny.
  When they asked, "Are you faint?"
  He replied, "No, I ain't,
But I'd rather I hadn't ate any!"

BRIAN O'LINN

This anonymous, nonsensical street ballad is from the seventeenth century.
The last verse is sometimes found in Mother Goose collections.

Brian O'Linn was a gentleman born,
His hair it was long and his beard unshorn,
His teeth were out and his eyes far in—
"I'm a wonderful beauty," says Brian O'Linn!

Brian O'Linn was hard up for a coat,
He borrowed the skin of a neighboring goat,
He buckled the horns right under his chin—
"They'll answer for pistols," says Brian O'Linn!

Brian O'Linn had no breeches to wear,
He got him a sheepskin to make him a pair,
With the fleshy side out and
   the woolly side in—
"They are pleasant and cool,"
   says Brian O'Linn!

Brian O'Linn had no hat to his head,
He stuck on a pot that was under the shed,
He murdered a cod for the sake of his fin—
"'Twill pass for a feather," says Brian O' Linn!

Brian O'Linn had no shirt to his back,
He went to a neighbor and borrowed a sack,
He puckered a meal-bag under his chin—
"They'll take it for ruffles," said Brian O'Linn!

Brian O'Linn had no shoes at all,
He bought an old pair at a cobbler's stall,
The uppers were broke and the soles were thin—
"They'll do me for dancing," says Brian O'Linn!

Brian O'Linn had no watch for to wear,
He bought a fine turnip and scooped it out fair,
He slipped a live cricket right under the skin—
"They'll think it is ticking," says Brian O'Linn!

Brian O'Linn was in want of a brooch,
He stuck a brass pin in a big cockroach,
The breast of his shirt he fixed it straight in—
"They'll think it's a diamond," says Brian O'Linn!

Brian O'Linn went a-courting one night,
He set both the mother and daughter to fight—

"Stop, stop," he exclaimed, "if you have but the tin*
I'll marry you both," says Brian O'Linn!

Brian O'Linn went to bring his wife home,
He had but one horse, that was all skin and bone—
"I'll put her behind me, as nate as a pin,
And her mother before me," says Brian O'Linn!

Brian O'Linn and his wife and wife's mother,
They all crossed over the bridge together,
The bridge broke down and they all tumbled in—
"We'll go home by water," says Brian O'Linn!

*Courage

FOLK RIDDLES

My daddy on the warm shelf,
Talking, talking to himself.   POT SIMMERING ON THE STOVE

A bottomless barrel shaped like a hive,
It's filled full of flesh, and the flesh is alive.   A THIMBLE

Up in the loft the round man lies,
Looking up through two hundred eyes.   A SIEVE

Out in the field my daddy grows,
Wearing his two hundred suits of clothes.

A BIG HEAD OF CABBAGE

From house to house he goes,
A messenger small and slight;
And whether it rains or snows,
He sleeps outside at night.   A LANE

I ran and I got,
I sat and I searched;
If I could get it
I would not bring it with me;
As I got it not, I brought it.   A THORN IN THE FOOT

A RIDDLE

Jonathan Swift

Can you find the five vowels in this poem?

We are little airy creatures,
All of different voice and features;
One of us in a glass is set,
One of us you'll find in jet.
T'other you may see in tin,
And the fourth a box within.
If the fifth you should pursue,
It can never fly from you.

IRISH OATHS AND CURSES

An Irish person, even when upset, is never at a loss for words.

"Six eggs to him, and a half of dozen of them rotten!"

"Sweet bad luck to her!"

"Good luck to him then, but may neither of
   them ever happen!"

"May she melt off the earth like snow off the ditch!"

"May he melt like butter before a summer sun!"

"May the devil swallow him sideways!"

"May she be afflicted with the itch and have no nails
   to scratch with!"

"Here's good health to your enemies' enemies!"

"May the grass grow before your door!" (Think about it.)

THE CURSE

John Millington Synge

John Millington Synge (1871-1909) was born and died near Dublin, and
wrote plays for the new Irish Theater.
Here he responds to a friend's sister who hated his latest play:

Lord, confound this surly sister,
Blight her brow with blotch and blister,
Cramp her larynx, lung, and liver,
In her guts a galling give her.

Let her live to earn her dinners
In Mountjoy* with seedy sinners:
Lord, this judgment quickly bring,
And I'm Your servant, J. M. Synge.

*A jail in Dublin

ANCIENT IRISH FOLK CURES

FOR CHILLS AND FEVER: Roll up a small live spider in a cobweb, put it into a lump of butter, and eat.

ANOTHER CURE FOR FEVER: Lie down on the sandy shore as the tide is coming in. The retreating waves will carry away the fever.

FOR A FEVER THAT LASTS NINE DAYS: Write the name of Jesus nine times on a slip of paper, cut the paper into small bits, mix the pieces with some soft food, and swallow it.

FOR STOMACHACHE: Tie a bunch of mint around your wrist.

FOR SIMPLE EARACHE: Take some wool from a black sheep and wear it constantly in the ear.

FOR DEAFNESS: Fold up two eels in a cabbage leaf, place them on the fire until they're soft, press out the juice, and drop it into the ears.

FOR FRECKLES: Anoint the freckled face with the blood of a bull or a rabbit.

FOR THE MUMPS: Wrap the child in a blanket, take it to the pigsty, rub the child's head to the back of a pig, and the mumps will pass from the child to the animal.

FOR DISEASES OF THE EYE: Pierce the shell of a living snail with a pin, take the fluid that comes out, and put it in the eyes.

FOR A STY ON THE EYELID: Point a gooseberry thorn at it nine times, saying, "Away, away, away!" The sty will disappear.

FOR WHOOPING COUGH: Put a trout into your mouth, then put it back alive into the stream. (A frog can be substituted.)

ANOTHER CURE FOR WHOOPING COUGH: Cut a lock of hair from the head of a person who never saw his father. Tie it in a piece of red cloth and wear around the neck.

TO CURE TONSILLITIS: Apply a stocking filled with hot potatoes to the throat.

TO CURE WARTS: Go to a funeral and take some of the clay from under the feet of the men who bear the coffin. Apply it to the wart, wishing strongly at the same time that it may disappear, and so it will be.

FOR TOOTHACHE: Go to a graveyard and kneel upon any grave. Say three prayers for the soul of the dead lying underneath. Take a handful of grass from the grave, chew it well, and spit it out without swallowing any. You will never have a toothache again.

HOW TO GO INVISIBLE: Get a raven's heart. Using a knife with a black handle, make three cuts in it and place a black bean in each cut. Then plant it, and when the beans sprout put one in your mouth and say, "I desire to be invisible," and so it will be as long as the bean is kept in the mouth.

PHILOSOPHIES FOR THE VERY YOUNG

Oscar Wilde

Known for his fairy tales and witty plays, Oscar Wilde was also famous for just walking around and being wickedly funny. Here he offers playful advice.

"If one tells the truth, one is sure, sooner or later, to be found out."

"One should either be a work of art, or wear a work of art."

"To love oneself is the beginning of a lifelong romance."

"The only way to make up for being a little overdressed is to be absolutely overeducated."

"The well-bred contradict other people. The wise contradict themselves."

"The old believe everything, the middle-aged suspect everything, the young know everything."

"One should always be a little improbable."

Erin go bragh! Ireland Forever!

SOURCE NOTES

All possible care has been taken to trace ownership of the selections and make full acknowledgment. If any errors or omissions have occurred, please notify the publisher and they will be corrected in future editions.

ONLY AN HOUR AWAY: *The Sea*

"The Enchanted Cap" found in many editions; it is believed to have first been collected by T. Crofton Croker and printed as "The Lady of Gollerus" in his *Fairy Legends of the South of Ireland* (1825). Croker, born in Cork in 1798, worked as a clerk and in his retirement collected stories on walking trips he took through Cork, Waterford, and Limerick. The Brothers Grimm immediately began translating Croker's work into German and made him internationally famous.

"All Day I Hear the Noise of Waters" from *Chamber Music* (1907), poems by James Joyce; also *1000 Years of Irish Poetry*, edited by Kathleen Hoagland (Old Greenwich, Conn.: The Devin-Adair Company, 1947).

"Herring Is King," first verse from a long poem of the same name, from *A Treasury of Irish Poetry*, edited by Stopford Brooke and T. W. Rolleston. (New York: Macmillan, 1905).

"Saint Patrick and the Salmon" or "The Flounder and the Salmon," from the oral tradition, recorded in county Cork (1932); collected by the Department of Irish Folklore, University College, Dublin, printed in *Legends from Ireland*, edited by Sean O'Sullivan (Totowa, New Jersey: Rowman and Littlefield, 1977).

"The Fate of the Children of Lir," translated from the Irish and collected by Lady Isabella Augusta Gregory in *Gods and Fighting Men* (1904). Gregory (1852–1932) was a writer and folklore collector, directed the Abbey Theater in Dublin, and frequently worked with William Butler Yeats (founding the Irish National Theater Society). Her home at Coole, county Galway, was a gathering place for Irish writers.

"Irish Lullaby" from *A Treasury of Irish Poetry*.

NOT JUST POTATOES: *The Food*

"Wheatlet, Son of Milklet," probably by a poor scholar or traveling poet of the Munster court named MacConglinne, who lived about 737 A.D. From *1000 Years of Irish Poetry*.

"Bewitched Butter," believed to have first been collected in county Donegal by Letitia Maclintock for *Dublin University Magazine* (1839), and then by William Butler Yeats in *Fairy and Folk Tales of the Irish Peasantry* (1888).

"Onions" and "Herrings" from *Verses for Fruit-women*, from Jonathan Swift's Collected Works (1795). From *1000 Years of Irish Poetry*.

"The Potato," collected in T. Crofton Croker's *Popular Songs of Ireland* (1837).

Irish Stew and other recipes adapted from various sources, including Theodora Fitzgibbon, *A Taste of Ireland* (London: Pan Books, 1968); Jeff Smith, *The Frugal Gourmet on Our Immigrant Ancestors* (New York: Avon, 1990); Dorothy and Thomas Hoobler, *The Irish American Family Album* (New York: Oxford, 1995).

ALIVE-ALIVE-O!: *The Music*

"The Musician's Invitation" from *Anglo-Irish Literature 1200–1582* by St. John D. Seymour (Cambridge: Cambridge University Press, 1929); later used by William Butler Yeats as a verse in his poem "I Am of Ireland."

"Larks" from *A Treasury of Irish Poetry*.

"Strings in the Earth and Air," from *Chamber Music* (1907) and *1000 Years of Irish Poetry*.

"The Traveling Men of Ballycoo," copyright © 1983 by Eve Bunting, reprinted by permission of Harcourt, Inc.

"Cockles and Mussels," from the eighteenth century, available in many sources. Though a bronze statue of Molly stands across the road from Trinity College, and Leopold Bloom, the hero of James Joyce's *Ulysses*, refers to her, she almost certainly was mythical, not real.

"The Fairies' Dancing Place," also known as "Lanty's New House." Believed to have first been collected from county Tyrone in William Carleton's *Tales and Stories of the Irish Peasantry* (1846), then by William Butler Yeats in *Irish Fairy Tales* (1892).

EMERALD ISLE: *The Pride*

"Saint Bridget Spreads Her Cloak," adapted from stories collected in county Wexford by Patrick Kennedy in *Legendary Fictions of the Irish Celts* (London: Macmillan, 1866), and Lady Isabella Augusta Gregory in *A Book of Saints and Wonders* (London: John Murray, 1907).

"The Limerick Lasses," a verse from a longer poem of the same name, from *A Treasury of Irish Poetry*.

"Finn McCool and the Scottish Giant," also known as "A Legend of Knockmany" and "The Giant's Causeway," collected by William Carleton in *Traits and Stories of the Irish Peasantry* (1830), then by William Butler Yeats in *Fairy and Folk Tales of the Irish Peasantry* (1888). Tales of Finn and the Fianna were much circulated in the third century A.D., with written accounts of them found even earlier.

"The Land of Eternal Youth," also known as "Usheen's Return to Ireland," collected in Galway by Lady Isabella Augusta Gregory in *The Kiltartan History Book* (1909). Usheen is spelled Oisin in Irish, and the Land of Eternal Youth is called Tir nan Og.

"Ireland" by Dora Sigerson, in various editions, including *A Rich and Rare Land: Irish Poetry and Paintings*, edited by Fleur Robertson (Surrey, U.K.: CLB International, 1994).

Irish Battle Cries, from various sources, including *A Treasury of Irish Folklore*, edited by Padraic Colum (New York: Kilkenny Press, 1954).

Irish Blessings, from various sources, including *Irish Blessings, Toasts, and Traditions*, edited by Jason Roberts (New York: Mercier Press, 1993). "Deep Peace" dates from 1150 A.D.

"All Things Bright and Beautiful," found in many editions.

IN LOVE WITH WORDS: *The Scholars*

For the role of Irish monks in world literature, see *How the Irish Saved Civilization: The Untold Story of Ireland's Heroic Role from the Fall of Rome to the Rise of Medieval Europe* by Thomas Cahill (New York: Doubleday, 1995).

"The Irish Student and His Cat," an anonymous poem that appears in many English versions, always stressing the uncanny similarities between students and cats.

"Ode to Writers" by Arthur O'Shaughnessy, many editions, including *1000 Years of Irish Poetry*.

"Where My Books Go," written in January 1892. Other Irish writers who won the Nobel Prize for literature in the twentieth century are Samuel Beckett, George Bernard Shaw, and Seamus Heaney.

"The Man Who Had No Story," recorded in County Cork 1933 by a storyteller who learned it from his mother seventy years earlier, collected in *Folktales of Ireland*, edited by Sean O'Sullivan (University of Chicago Press, 1966) and in other books. Over a hundred versions of this humorous, nightmarish fantasy have been recorded in Ireland.

FIELDS AND FARMS: *The Land*

"The Wind That Shakes the Barley" from *A Rich and Rare Land: Irish Poetry and Paintings*.

"Donald O'Neary and His Neighbors" found in many editions. It was a popular part of the oral tradition, believed to have first been collected in *Royal Hibernian Tales* (1825) and by William Butler Yeats in *Fairy and Folk Tales of the Irish Peasantry*.

"The Lake Isle of Innisfree," written 1890. Sometimes Yeats saw himself as a dashing hero of adventurous love stories, sometimes as living all alone on an island. One day while walking on a busy city street feeling ". . . very homesick, I heard a little tinkle of water and saw a fountain in a shop window which balanced a little ball upon its jet, and began to remember lake water. . . ." From the memory came this poem.

"My Land" in various editions, including *A Rich and Rare Land: Irish Poetry and Paintings*.

ENCHANTMENT: *The Fairies*

"The Fairies in New Ross," anonymous, from Wexford County, early nineteenth century, found in many editions.

"The Fairies," also known as "A Child's Song," written at Killybegs in 1849 and published in Allingham's *Poems*, 1850. The places mentioned are ones he knew from childhood.

"Fair, Brown, and Trembling" found in many editions, first collected by Jeremiah Curtin in 1887 and published in *Myths and Folk-Lore of Ireland* (Boston: Little, Brown, and Company, 1890). Curtin, the American son of Irish immigrants, collected stories from Galway, Kerry, Limerick, and Donegal, as well as from the 2,000 volumes of Gaelic folklore in Dublin libraries (known as the richest trove of myths in Europe).

"The Stolen Child" first appeared in the *Irish Monthly*, December 1886. It marked Yeats's decision to write poetry only on Irish subjects. Of it Yeats wrote: "The places mentioned are round about Sligo. Further, Rosses is a very noted fairy locality. . . . A little point of rocks where, if anyone falls asleep, there is danger of their waking silly, the fairies having carried off their souls."

"To Cure a Child Under a Fairy Spell," from *Irish Cures, Mystic Charms, and Superstitions of Ireland* (Boston: Ticknor and Co., 1887) by Lady Wilde (1820–1896), who used "Speranza" as her pseudonym and was the mother of Oscar.

"The Star-Child," adapted from *The Happy Prince and Other Tales* (1888) and various editions of the complete works of Oscar Wilde.

WHO MAKES THE FAIRIES' SHOES?: *The Leprechauns*

"Patrick O'Donnell and the Leprechaun," apparently first published in Croker's *Fairy Legends of the South of Ireland*, now the most reprinted of all leprechaun stories.

"The Leprechaun," by William Allingham, in Yeats's *Fairy and Folk Tales of the Irish Peasantry* and many editions.

"The Leprechaun," by Robert Dwyer Joyce, in *The Irish Leprechaun Book* by Mary Feehan (New York: Mercier Press, 1994) and many editions.

PEOPLE NEVER STOP TALKING: *The Blarney*

On the first use of *blarney* in the modern sense by Queen Elizabeth, see Anthony Butler, *The Book of Blarney* (New York: Bell Publishing, 1969). Nonsense verse from "The Soul Cages," a story collected by T. Crofton Croker in *Legends of the Lakes* (1829).

Limericks, thanks to Paul Brewer and his collection of two hundred joke books.

"Brian O'Linn," collected by Paul McCall, *The Humor of Ireland* (London: Walter Scott, 1894).

Folk Riddles from various sources, including *A Treasury of Irish Folklore*, edited by Padraic Colum (New York: Kilkenny Press, 1954), and in collections by Douglas Hyde (1860–1949) and Francis Fahy (1854–1931).

"A Riddle," from *1000 Years of Irish Poetry*.

Irish Oaths and Curses, from various sources, including William Carleton, *Traits and Stories of the Irish Peasantry* (1830).

Ancient Irish Folk Cures, mostly from *Irish Cures, Mystic Charms, and Superstitions of Ireland.*

"Philosophies for the Very Young," adapted from "Phrases and Philosophies for the Use of the Young" by Oscar Wilde, first published in the December 1894 issue of *Chameleon*.

ACKNOWLEDGMENTS

Much appreciation to the following for help:
My father, Kenneth Krull, for shipping so quickly the Ireland books of my mother,
Helen Folliard Krull; my aunts Sister Dorothy Folliard and Donna Folliard; Maureen
and Colette Lyons for use of their "Holiday Home" in Ballyduff in county Kerry;
James O'Connor, Mary Scannell, and Tony Quinn; the librarians at the San Diego
Public Library; Alessandra Balzer; Helen Foster James; Vicky Reed; Eve Bunting;
Sheila Cole; Susan Malk of the White Rabbit bookstore; and Peter Neumeyer.
—K.K.

I would like to thank all of the Irish people who allowed me
(knowingly, or not) to draw and photograph their fields, farms, and faces.
If you let me (and even if you don't) I'll be back.
Also, thanks to Jaime Myers, photographer, for the use of her many pictures
of the Irish coast and the sea (the check is in the mail!).
—D.McP.

Compilation and adaptations copyright © 2004 by Kathleen Krull
Illustrations copyright © 2004 by David McPhail

For information address Disney • Hyperion Books, 114 Fifth Avenue, New York, New York 10011-5690.
First Disney • Hyperion paperback edition, 2009
10 9 8 7 6 5 4 3 2 1
ISBN 978-1-4231-1752-0

Library of Congress Cataloging-in-Publication Data on file.
Designed by Christine Kettner
Printed in Singapore
Visit www.hyperionbooksforchildren.com